SWITZERLAND
THE SUMMIT OF EUROPE

DISCOVERING our HERITAGE

by Margaret Schrepfer

DILLON PRESS, INC.
Minneapolis, Minnesota 55415

To the Detroit Swiss Society

Photographic Acknowledgments

The photographs are reproduced through the courtesy of the California State Library, Michigan State Art Library, Margaret Schrepfer, the Swiss National Tourist Office, and Lee Taylor. Cover photograph by Albert Moldvay.

Library of Congress Cataloging-in-Publication Data
Schrepfer, Margaret.
   Switzerland, the summit of Europe / Margaret Schrepfer.
     p. cm. — (Discovering our heritage)
   Bibliography; p.
   Includes index.
   Summary: Describes the history, geographical features, family life, traditions, food, celebrations, and industry of Switzerland, as well as its four ethnic groups and their languages.
   ISBN 0-87518-405-7
   1. Switzerland—Juvenile literature. [1. Switzerland.]
I. Title. II. Series.
DQ17.S287   1989
949.4—dc19   88-35913
                                                               CIP
                                                                AC

© 1989 by Dillon Press, Inc. All rights reserved

Dillon Press, Inc., 242 Portland Avenue South
Minneapolis, Minnesota 55415

Printed in the United States of America
1 2 3 4 5 6 7 8 9 10 98 97 96 95 94 93 92 91 90 89

Contents

	Fast Facts about Switzerland	4
	Map of Switzerland	6
1	The Heart of Europe	7
2	The Swiss Melting Pot	24
3	A Long Way to Peace	37
4	The International Nation	50
5	William Tell and Other Tales	60
6	Celebrating Swiss Style	72
7	Chalets, Cheese, and Chocolate	86
8	Education, the Swiss Way	101
9	The World's Playground	108
10	To Begin Again	118
	Appendix A: Swiss Cantons	129
	Appendix B: The Official Languages of Switzerland	130
	Appendix C: Swiss Consulates in the United States and Canada	131
	Glossary	133
	Selected Bibliography	138
	Index	139

Fast Facts about Switzerland

Official Name: Schweiz (in German); Suisse (in French); Svizzera (in Italian)

Official Languages: German, French, Italian (Romansh is a national language)

Capital: Bern

Location: In Central Europe, bordered by Germany on the north, Italy on the south, France on the west, and Liechtenstein and Austria on the east

Area: 15,941 square miles (41,288 square kilometers); *greatest distances:* north-south—138 miles (222 kilometers); east-west—213 miles (343 kilometers)

Elevation: *Highest*—15,203 feet (4,634 meters) above sea level at Dufourspitze of Monte Rosa; *lowest*—633 feet (193 meters) at Lake Maggiore

Population: 6,551,000 (1988 estimate); *distribution*—60 percent urban, 40 percent rural; *density*—410 persons per square mile (159 persons per square kilometer)

Form of Government: Federal republic; a president elected by the Federal Assembly is the head of government; political powers are divided between the central government and the cantonal, or state, government

Important Products: Chemicals, electrical equipment, watches, textiles, dairy products (cheese), and chocolate
Basic Unit of Money: Swiss franc
Major Religions: Roman Catholic and Protestant
Flag: Red flag with a large white cross in the center
National Anthem: Schweizer Psalm (Swiss Hymn)
Major Holidays: New Year's Day—January 1; Epiphany—January 6; Good Friday; Easter; Easter Monday; Swiss National Day—August 1; Pfingsten Monday (Pentecost); All Saints' Day—November 1; Christmas Day—December 25

1. The Heart of Europe

For people around the world, Switzerland is a storybook land of snow-capped peaks, mountain meadows bursting with wildflowers, fertile valleys dotted with picturesque castles and villages, and crystal clear lakes. It is the fairy-tale land of Heidi and William Tell, of hand-carved clocks and picture-perfect homes, of men and women in colorful traditional clothes. These are the images many people have when they think of Switzerland.

This larger-than-life European nation does have an abundance of mountains and lakes, valleys and villages. Yet it is also a modern country where most of the people live in cities. Some large cities, such as Zurich, Geneva, and Basel, are as crowded as New York City, while some villages have fewer than twenty houses. Modern apartment buildings stand beside 500-year-old castles. While young people often dress in blue jeans, older people may dress in clothes similar to those the Swiss wore a hundred years ago. Switzerland is now known for its high-speed trains and international banks as well as its beautiful mountains and valleys. It is also known as the host for a growing number of international organizations and as a meeting place where

Wildflowers bloom along a swiftly flowing stream in a mountain meadow in the upper Engadine area of Switzerland.

representatives gather to discuss global issues and to settle disputes among nations.

Switzerland has made a name for itself around the world as a peaceful country that will not take sides in conflicts among nations. Because Switzerland is neutral, it is a place where many of the world's powers feel safe to discuss world politics. The Swiss have worked hard to make their nation an island of security in a troubled world.

At the Bernina Pass in eastern Switzerland, a train of the Bernina Railway passes by Lake Bianco.

A Land of Many Faces

Located in central Europe, Switzerland is often called the "heart of Europe." Only half the size of Maine, this small country can be crossed by car in less than a day. It is one of the few European nations that is completely landlocked, or surrounded by other countries. On the northern border is Germany, to the south is Italy, to the west is France, and to the east are Liechtenstein and Austria.

Switzerland shares the languages of its surrounding neighbors and is, in fact, like several different countries all in one. The Swiss have three official languages: German, French, and Italian. An unofficial, but national, language is the ancient, Latin-based Romansh. Signs

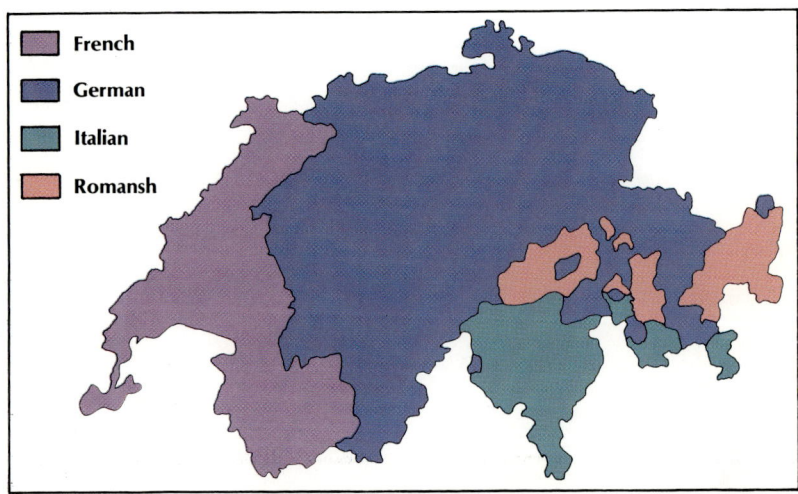

Swiss Language Regions

High in the Alps, hikers climb a mountain path.

throughout Switzerland may be printed in several languages, and the Swiss often speak three or more languages themselves.

Just as the Swiss are divided into language groups, the land is divided into different geographic regions. The Alps, a mountainous area located in southern Switzerland, forms the country's largest region. The Mittelland, the "middle land," lies between the Alps and the Jura, the northernmost region of the country. The Jura, famous for its Jura Mountains, is the smallest region of Switzerland.

The Alps

The mountains of the Alps form a natural barrier between the northern European countries and Italy on the Mediterranean Sea. Winding passes cut through the mountains have allowed centuries of wanderers to cross the rocky land. The Saint Gotthard Pass forms a central junction of four mountain chains. Here, more than a hundred trains and thousands of cars travel each day through one of the world's longest tunnels.

Another famous pass is the Great Saint Bernard Pass. In 1050 A.D., a monk named Bernard of Menthon established a shelter for travelers. This area was dangerous to travel through, so the monks raised a special breed of dogs to help travelers in distress. These huge, intelligent dogs, now known as Saint Bernards, have a keen sense of smell and are good at finding people lost in the snow. In the early 1800s, one dog named Barry saved more than forty people from freezing to death.

In the mountains, rain, sleet, or snow falls frequently, and the weather is a source of much Swiss conversation. On a warm sunny day, the Swiss may say, "This is real headache weather. The wind will surely bring fire to the mountain villages." The wind they are talking about is called the *Föhn*. People and animals feel restless several hours before it actually comes. Everything far away looks closer; in fact, some

Every year, millions of skiers from around the world travel to the Swiss Alps to test their skill on the snow-covered slopes.

Swiss say they can count the rocks on distant mountaintops! The Föhn comes from the south and causes temperatures to rise quickly. Sometimes it sparks fires and can make a village burn.

The heavy snowfall on the peaks of the Swiss Alps draws millions of skiers to the region every year. In the spring, summer, and fall, people come from all over the world to climb mountains and hike along the thousands of trails.

On the southern side of the mountains, the weather is usually mild. Swiss Italian towns such as Locarno and Lugano have become winter resorts for many Swiss, just as certain cities in Florida and California are for many Americans. This area of palm trees and blooming flowers seems far removed from the snowy mountains of the Alps.

The Alps are important to the Swiss for more than beauty and recreation. Their huge, snow-covered peaks provide the country with a vital resource—water. Switzerland has more than a thousand lakes and many rivers. Four of Europe's major rivers are born in the Alps: the Rhine, the Rhône, the Ticino, and the Inn. The Ticino River joins the Po River, and the Inn River joins the Danube River before they flow into the sea hundreds of miles south of their sources. The Rhine River flows north through Europe and empties into the North Sea, while the Rhône River flows into the Mediterranean Sea.

The Swiss need their water resources to produce energy, because their land has no fossil fuels such as crude oil. The rushing mountain rivers, fueled by melted snow and ice, provide power for hydroelectric stations. These stations produce about three-fourths of Switzerland's electric power. Nuclear power plants, however, supply an increasing amount of energy for the country's growing needs.

The Rhine, one of Europe's major rivers, flows through the Swiss city of Basel and on to the North Sea.

The Mittelland

One area in which the Swiss cannot meet their own needs is agriculture. There simply isn't enough land, and what is available for farming is valuable and expensive. If a farm is owned by a family, the property is proudly passed on from generation to generation. Some farms stay in the same family for hundreds of years.

Although many farms are located in the valleys beneath the Alps, the real breadbasket of the country

The rolling plains of the Swiss Mittelland provide valuable farmland in a country known for its scenic mountains.

lies on the rolling plains of the Swiss Plateau, in the region called the Mittelland. This is the second largest region in Switzerland, and two-thirds of the population live in its cities and on its farms.

Bern, a Swiss German town in the Mittelland, is the capital of Switzerland and the seat of Swiss government. Inside the capitol building, or the *Bundeshaus*, members of the two parliamentary houses of the Federal Assembly meet to make governmental decisions.

The Swiss do not have a powerful central government. Many political decisions are made by all twenty-

The Bundeshaus (House of Parliament) *in Bern.*

six cantons, which include four half-cantons. Cantons are something like states in America. Each has its own government, whose rights are guaranteed by the national constitution.

The Federal Assembly, made up of cantonal representatives, elects the Federal Council and the president. The president, who serves as a kind of chairperson, can only be elected to office for one year at a time. During the term, the Swiss president can walk freely on the streets with no bodyguard, and can take the trolley or train like anyone else, often without even being recognized. Some Swiss might know the name of the president of the United States before that of their own.

Near Bern's capitol building lie flowers and brightly painted fountains, and a giant clock tower with moving figures. Old Bern, located in the central part of the city, is surrounded on three sides by the Aare River. The *Bärengraben*, or bear pit, has attracted visitors to this area since the end of the eighteenth century. The bear is the city's symbol, and *bären* is the German word for "bears." Visitors come to the Bärengraben to see the brown bears stand up by the high cement block walls.

Zurich, Switzerland's largest city, is the economic, industrial, and cultural center of the country. The city lies near Lake Zurich, and is built on both sides of the River Limmat. The main street and the center of Zurich's activity is the *Bahnhofstrasse*, which stretches from

The elegant shops and large banks of the Bahnhofstrasse *have helped make Zurich a well-known shopping and banking center.*

the train station to the lake. Here, elegant shops full of watches, clocks, jewelry, and clothing attract eager shoppers from all over the world.

The Bahnhofstrasse is also the banking center of Switzerland. The Swiss are known to be thrifty people, and their personal savings are the highest in Europe. Many people also come from outside of the country to deposit their money in banks along the Bahnhofstrasse. Two-fifths of the bank accounts in Zurich are held by foreign investors, who like the secrecy and stability of the Swiss banks.

Whether for business or pleasure, about a million tourists a year visit Zurich. The city has a large international airport and a railroad station to help transport the visitors. The Swiss are famous for their efficient transportation systems, and some say that they can set their watches by the prompt arrivals of the Swiss trains.

The Swiss work hard to develop their industries as well. Zurich produces textiles, medical instruments, large generators, and Lindt chocolate. The Swiss Institute of Technology and the University of Zurich provide training and education for people who want to work in these industries.

The city of Geneva, located in the western, French-speaking tip of Switzerland, is an exciting, beautiful, international city. It lies in the hills along the southwest end of Lake Geneva, or Lac Léman. The Rhône River flows by Geneva's historic buildings, fountains, and winding streets. Huge parks and marble buildings add to the city's beauty.

Geneva is not only a commercial, industrial, and financial center in Switzerland, but is also an international meeting ground. Although Switzerland is not a member of the United Nations, Geneva's *Palais des Nations*, or Palace of Nations, is the European headquarters for the organization. In large assembly halls, speeches can be translated immediately into English, French, Spanish, Russian, and Chinese.

The Jura

The Jura lies along the western edge of the country and is the smallest region in the country, making up only about one-tenth of Switzerland. The Jura Mountains are lower in elevation than the Alps, and are covered with trees that provide much of the lumber needed by the Swiss. Several major industrial cities, such as Basel, are located in the Jura.

Originally built on both sides of the Rhine River as a Roman fortress, Basel is now the second largest city in Switzerland. Ancient buildings are a common sight in Basel. One of the oldest, a church called the *Münster*, dates back to the ninth century. Its twin red sandstone spires tower from the city's highest point.

Yet Basel is also a city of modern banks, businesses, and factories. Basel's factories produce chemicals, medicines, machinery, and electrical equipment. Ciba-Geigy, the world's largest chemical company, is located here, along with many other chemical warehouses and plants.

Basel has developed into an important center of trade and business mainly because of its location on the Swiss border along the Rhine River. Today, families in low, bargelike boats—carrying mostly food and petroleum products—travel up the Rhine from the Netherlands on the North Sea. Often, laundry hangs on a line

Entire families live on the bargelike boats that travel up and down the Rhine between the Netherlands and Switzerland.

strung between the front and the back of the boat, while children play or ride small bicycles on the deck.

Some of the towns in the Jura are large watchmaking centers. Neuchâtel, for example, is an important research center where Swiss scientists develop new watch and clock designs. Switzerland was the world's leader in the watch industry until the 1970s, when Japan and the United States began to produce large numbers of quartz watches. In the 1980s, however, the Swiss watchmakers made a comeback when they developed an inexpensive quartz watch called the Swatch. Set in brightly colored plastic with matching bands, the watch became an instant success. Ever since its introduction, it has sold well in stores around the world.

The Swiss try hard to keep their country running smoothly. Although the Swiss differ greatly from region to region, from canton to canton, they all share a pride in their successful industries, elegant cities, and beautiful landscapes.

2. The Swiss Melting Pot

The people of Switzerland are as varied as their mountains. For centuries, warlike invaders from Germany, France, and Italy came to conquer the land. People from all over the world still come to Switzerland, but in peaceful search of a neutral meeting ground, recreation, or business opportunities. Today, Switzerland prides itself in its leading role as an international center.

Swiss Citizens—Old and New

New people entering Switzerland bring in fresh ideas and traditions. More than a million of the country's residents today came from foreign countries. They are much-needed additions to the Swiss labor force, since Switzerland has more jobs available than its own people can fill. Workers from Italy, Greece, Yugoslavia, Spain, and Turkey have traveled to Switzerland to find work, or in some cases to flee from political oppression.

Life is not always easy for new immigrants, partly because of Switzerland's citizenship laws. In the United States, residents are first a citizen of their country, then of their state, and last of their community. Swiss citizenship works in just the opposite way. The Swiss are

Many Swiss have strong ties to their local communities and traditions. These young men and women dress in traditional costumes for a folklore festival at Burgdorf in the Bernese Mittelland.

first citizens of their community, and last of their country. This custom dates back to the thirteenth century. If a Swiss is a citizen of a certain community, it does not mean that the person lives or was born there. The origin or place of citizenship may date back several generations.

Because of these citizenship laws, many foreign workers have to live alone until their families can legally join them. Decent housing at an affordable cost can be hard to find. In addition to these difficulties, new immigrants must face a new country, language, customs, and often prejudice.

The Swiss Languages

More than half of the Swiss speak many versions of a German dialect called *Schwyzerdütsch*, or Swiss German. This language is spoken in eastern, central, and northern Switzerland, but is not written. High German, or *Hochdeutsch*, is the language that students learn in school. Swiss German differs from high German. Its local dialects can vary from one area to another within the country. People living in Bern call a potato *Herdöpfel*, but the people of Thurgau call it *Gümeli*.

In western Switzerland, many Swiss speak French, and in the southern part, many speak Italian. The French and Italian Swiss are affected the most by the

The Swiss Melting Pot 27

Swiss language barriers, largely because they are outnumbered by the Swiss Germans. Because it is impossible to understand all of the Schwyzerdütsch dialects, some think that the different cantons should speak only high German. But the Swiss Germans do not agree because they want to preserve their Swiss German heritage.

One percent of the population speaks an ancient language called Romansh, which is spoken mainly in the canton of Graubünden in eastern Switzerland. Romansh is kept alive by a small number of people who are enthusiastic about preserving the disappearing language.

Roles and Duties

Change does not come easily to the Swiss. Just as they try to preserve their different languages, they uphold social roles that haven't changed much in the last two hundred years. For example, it is still common for a woman to stay home with her family after she is married, rather than to go to work. Taking care of children, cooking, and cleaning are referred to as "making a household." Many Swiss women take great care to maintain a clean, well-run home.

However, an increasing number of young women are looking for jobs. As more women join the work

Some cantons still hold large outdoor gatherings, called the

force, they gain a larger voice in Swiss society. In 1971, women were finally granted the right to vote in national elections. In one canton, women still cannot vote in local elections.

Women's rights were so slow in coming partly because for many years most Swiss women felt that voting was unnecessary for them. Whatever law they wanted to pass, they would persuade their male family members to vote for it. They claimed that although the men may have ruled Switzerland, the women ruled the men.

Landsgemeinde, *where citizens vote by raising a hand.*

Still, Switzerland is a country where men have strong leadership roles—at home and in the community. Besides working at a full-time job, a man has numerous duties such as serving in the Swiss army and participating in local city meetings and elections. In a few cantons, tax and school policies are decided during a big outdoor meeting called the *Landsgemeinde.* There, each person votes for or against proposals by raising a hand. Many Swiss believe that political responsibilities make a man more manly.

The Serious Swiss

A good public image is important to most Swiss, and they take themselves seriously. Sometimes when Americans do something wrong or foolish, they will joke about it. The Swiss do not often laugh at themselves, although they might laugh at something their neighbor has done. Part of keeping a good public image for the Swiss is self-control. For example, they believe that it is not polite to show anger in front of other people. If they are not happy with someone else, they may complain to their family, but not directly to the person.

The Swiss are industrious people, with great respect for quality work. They believe that they will not be happy unless they are constantly working or doing something constructive. Children learn to work early in life. Hours of chores and homework give them little time for play after school.

When they are not working, the Swiss are often making crafts. Such crafts as embroidery work, hand-painted plates and plaques, woodcarvings, pottery, handspun yarns, and weavings are made throughout Switzerland. However, even their craftmaking has a practical end. Homemade crafts are sold in *Heimatwerk* (homework) stores that are located in cities throughout the country.

Jass and Wanderwege

Everybody works hard, but the Swiss do take time for recreation, too. In some families, a card game called *Jass* is played in the evenings or on Sunday afternoons. A Jass deck has four brightly colored suits: acorns, bells, flowers, and shields. In this game, players add numbers, which is one reason the Swiss are fast in mental arithmetic.

Another favorite Swiss pastime is hiking in the mountains. Weather permitting, many families put on their hiking clothes and hiking boots, and pack a picnic lunch in their rucksacks (backpacks). Then they drive or take a train to the nearest mountain and spend the day walking on the well-marked *Wanderwege* (footpaths). Many Swiss have highly technical jobs, and they enjoy getting away to a beautiful natural setting.

Switzerland's Great Thinkers

Even though Switzerland is a small country, it has produced a large number of people who have made important contributions in many fields such as psychology, philosophy, art, music, and literature.

Two famous Swiss psychologists are Carl Jung (1875-1961) and Jean Piaget (1896-1980). Carl Jung was the founder of analytical psychology. He believed

that psychology is the science of the future because people are more threatened by people than by disease or natural disaster. Jung believed that through psychology, people can learn to understand themselves and others.

Jean Piaget, one of the world's foremost child psychologists, spent much of his life watching children to understand how they think, learn, and grow into adults. He formed some of his opinions by watching his own three children, and wrote many books on child development. Today, Piaget's ideas are taught in nearly every university in the United States.

Another famous Swiss is Jean-Jacques Rousseau, a philosopher who believed in the natural goodness of people. He loved freedom and hated tyranny. Rousseau felt that people acted in evil ways because their political and social situations were evil. He thought that teachers should encourage self-expression rather than training students with harsh discipline. He said, "Might never makes right." Because the government disapproved of his beliefs, he had to flee Switzerland, and he lived in France for much of his life.

Art, Music, and Literature

Switzerland has long contributed its creative talents to many fields, and the country's beauty has inspired

A Swiss family hikes on a trail overlooking Lake Brienz in the Bernese Alps.

artists for centuries. Swiss artist Konratt Witz was one of the first to paint realistic-looking landscapes. After him, many other Swiss followed, including Ferdinand Hodler (1835-1918), Giovanni Segantini (1858-1889), and Albert Anker (1831-1910).

Paul Klee (1879-1940), a twentieth-century artist, is highly regarded in the art world. He painted dreamlike pictures, called surrealistic, which means that they show something that isn't real. Since the Swiss tend to be conservative and don't accept new ideas easily, many do not like his paintings.

Music is also important to the Swiss, who have added their talents to the music world. Two great twentieth-century Swiss composers were Ernest Bloch (1880-1959) and Arthur Honegger (1892-1955). In the early part of the century, Ernest Bloch came from Geneva to the United States. He had a great influence over the development of serious music, and was best known for works that reflected his Jewish heritage. Bloch composed several symphonies, including *Helvetia*, expressing his love for his native Switzerland, and *American Symphony*, in honor of his adopted country. Arthur Honegger, a composer of modern music, was born in France, but was legally Swiss. One of his most famous works is *Jeanne d'Arc au bucher*, or "Joan of Arc at the Stake."

Switzerland has produced many authors, and one

A Swiss grandfather sits by the hut on the "Heidi Alp."

of the most well known is Johann David Wyss (1743-1818), the author of *Swiss Family Robinson*. This book, written in 1813, describes the adventures of a shipwrecked family. Another Swiss story that is well loved around the world is *Heidi*, written in 1881 by Johanna Spyri (1827-1901).

Heidi is a story, perhaps based in fact, of an orphan girl who lived with her grandfather on a high pasture of a mountain just above the village of Dörfli. Today, a small building that fits the description of Grandfather's hut lies on the "Heidi Alp," a high mountain pasture above the town of Rofels. The door of the hut is always open, and anybody can go in and sign the guest book that lies on a long wooden table. If you have a backpack and carry your sleeping bag up the steep climb from Rofels, you can sleep in the loft and see the sky as Heidi saw it.

When you see all that beauty, you can understand why Switzerland has produced so many thinkers, musicians, artists, and writers. Switzerland is a country whose greatest natural resource is its people.

3. A Long Way to Peace

No one knows exactly when the first people came to the land that is now Switzerland. However, records do show that short, stocky, cave-dwelling, bear-hunting men and women known as Neanderthals wandered there from about 35,000 to 100,000 years ago. At different times during this period, large glaciers covered the land, and the huge ice packs made the land unfriendly to traveling nomadic tribes. When the last ice age came, the Neanderthals and the cave bears disappeared.

As the ice began to melt, the land became more appealing to wanderers. Thick forests and rich fields provided good food sources, and the looming mountains protected the valleys. During the period called the Stone Age, Neolithic people began to settle down, raise animals, grow plants, and make tools and pots. They lived in huts perched on pilings, or wooden poles, along lakeshores. Small settlements formed clusters on the plateaus beneath the mountains.

Attacks on All Sides

Roaming tribes continued to travel the land for hundreds of years. By 500 B.C., a large tribe called the

Helvetians had settled in the region. The Helvetians weren't the only tribe on the land. The Rhaeti, a group from northern Italy, lived along the mountain passes. The two groups lived there together until powerful tribes from Germany tried to take over the land. The Helvetians decided that they would rather leave their homes than fight the Germans, so they planned a mass migration to France. In 58 B.C., a long line of men, women, children, and cattle headed west for the Atlantic coast of southern France.

Julius Caesar, the Roman general who ruled over Italy, southern France, and most of Europe, did not want the Helvetians wandering across his territory. He rushed from Rome to Geneva, where he organized six legions of soldiers and quickly defeated the Alpine tribespeople. The Helvetians were forced to return to their homeland. To make sure that they stayed home, Caesar set up military posts with several thousand Roman soldiers.

The Romans heavily influenced the Swiss. They built towns with palaces, amphitheaters, and temples. The remains of these structures are still scattered across Switzerland. The Romans built roads which crisscrossed the country, including the first road over the Great Saint Bernard Pass. They also improved farming techniques and began to cultivate vineyards, such as those located along the shores of Lake Geneva.

A Long Way to Peace

Christianity was first introduced to the tribespeople at this time, as was the Latin language of the Roman conquerors. Today, the Romansh language closely resembles Latin. Also, the Latin word *Helvetia* appears on all official documents and on all Swiss currency and stamps. Swiss license plates carry the code CH, which stands for *Confederatio Helvetica,* or "Swiss Confederation."

Power Changes Hands

The Romans ruled Switzerland for the next four hundred years. But they had to withdraw their troops in order to defend Italy from the Huns, a warlike tribe from the east. With the Romans gone, the French Burgundians and the German Alemanni attacked the land from both sides. They soon conquered the territory, but the two groups ruled the Swiss in different ways.

The Burgundians, who had been living under Roman rule for a long time, did not make many changes in the laws, so life went on as usual for the tribespeople. But few liked the Alemanni. They destroyed peaceful villages, killing the remaining Romans and many of the Helvetians. Those not killed were forced to learn the Alemanni language and customs. The Helvetians rebelled several times against the Alemanni, without success.

It was not until the arrival of the Frankish Emperor Charlemagne (Charles the Great) in the second half of the eighth century that the harsh rule of the Alemanni was finally broken. Charlemagne ruled over the Holy Roman Empire, or what is now a large part of western Europe. Life under Charlemagne's rule was an improvement for the people of the villages. He raised the standard of living for all, and created more interest in education, literature, and philosophy.

After Charlemagne died, the land came under the influence of the Holy Roman Empire, but it was controlled by selfish, powerful families such as the Habsburgs. These nobles made their own laws and levied heavy taxes. Such unfair treatment was more than the village peasants could stand. They had been willing to accept the authority of the emperor, but not that of the local rulers and tax collectors.

The Eternal Pact

Representatives from what are now the forest cantons of Uri, Schwyz, and Unterwalden (now Nidwalden and Obwalden) met August 1, 1291, on a pasture called the Rütli above the shores of Lake Lucerne. There they formed the "eternal pact," promising to help each other in the struggle against the Habsburgs. They also declared their right to make their own laws in the pact,

Each year thousands of people walk up a steep path from Lake Lucerne to visit the historic pasture called the Rütli.

which would be the foundation of the Swiss Confederation. Today, August 1 is celebrated as Swiss National Day, and the Rütli is a national shrine. Even though it can only be reached by boat and by walking up a steep path, thousands of people visit the historic pasture each year.

Fighting for the Confederation

Many years of rebellion against the Habsburgs followed the formation of the eternal pact. In 1315, the Habsburg Duke Leopold III sent an Austrian army of 20,000 men to fight the Swiss, who had only 1,200 men in their army. As the duke's army approached a town called Morgarten, the men from the three forest cantons stationed themselves in the surrounding hills. When the duke's army advanced, the Swiss rolled rocks and boulders down on the invaders. In less than two hours, 1,500 Austrians were killed. The others fled in terror. This is still proudly remembered as the first Confederation victory.

The Confederation, now called *Schweiz* after the canton of Schwyz, was gaining ground. Five more cantons joined, and rich and poor alike banded together to attack the Austrians. The Swiss looted and burned their castles; no Austrian soldier or Habsburg was safe from their violent attacks.

A Long Way to Peace

Duke Leopold, who was shamefully defeated at Morgarten, decided to put down the Swiss once and for all. He sent more than 20,000 men into Switzerland. At Sempach, the Austrian army fought the first battle against an army of 1,500 Swiss peasants. Duke Leopold was sure of victory. He rode out in front of his men showing the rope with which he was going to hang the Swiss. With their new long spears, the Austrians thought they could conquer the Swiss, who were armed only with axes and long clubs.

They were mistaken, because at this point Arnold von Winkelried of Unterwalden rushed out against the Austrians' spears. He grabbed as many of them in his arms as he could. Pierced with many wounds, he fell. History has it that his last words were, "Confederates, I will open you a path. Take care of my wife and children." Arnold von Winkelried is still a national hero. The Swiss defeated Leopold at Sempach, and today, the Chapel of Saint Jakob stands on that site, honoring the brave Swiss soldiers who fought there.

The Tamers of Kings

Throughout the terrible wars between Switzerland and Austria, the Swiss became widely known as fierce fighters with excellent marksmanship. Their famed reputation as "tamers of kings" spread. Other countries began hiring Swiss soldiers to fight their wars. They fought and defeated Europe's strongest monarchs, including France's powerful leader, Charles the Bold. They drove the French out of northern Italy. All those soldiers of fortune eventually threatened the Confederation because the Swiss ended up fighting against each other in different armies. Later, in the sixteenth century, Switzerland passed a law forbidding its citizens to be hired out as soldiers. That law remained in effect for almost two hundred years.

The Swiss Fight the Swiss

During the last part of the fifteenth century, the Swiss began to quarrel among themselves over which territories should be admitted into the Confederation. One of their biggest arguments concerned the towns of Fribourg and Solothurn. The country peasants opposed their entry into the Confederation, and held many demonstrations to protest it.

At the point of civil war, Niklaus von Flüe appeared before the council, the *Diet*, and persuaded the Swiss leaders to settle their differences by compromise rather than by fighting another war. He advised the people to admit the towns on the conditions that they give up their separate alliances to other countries, and that they remain neutral in any conflict that might

A memorial fountain with a statue of Niklaus von Flüe stands before the parish church in Sachseln.

divide the eight cantons. Von Flüe contributed to the beginning of Switzerland's policy of neutrality, and was later honored as a patron saint, or special protector, of Switzerland.

When the Catholic Holy Roman Empire formally recognized Switzerland as an independent country in 1648, there were still only nine cantons. Nine-tenths of the peasants lived in extreme povery. Again, they had to give what little money they earned for taxes to the nobles. In 1653, they tried to revolt, but they lost, and many were put to death.

The Reformation

During the sixteenth century, a movement against Catholicism known as the Reformation swept through Europe. In 1517, Martin Luther, a German priest, protested certain practices and fundamental beliefs of the Catholic Church. Luther's ideas for church reform inspired other religious leaders, including a Swiss priest named Huldreich Zwingli.

Although Zwingli agreed with some of Luther's ideas, the Swiss reformer developed a Protestant doctrine that differed from Lutheranism. For instance, Zwingli believed in the right of the lay people rather than the clergy to control the church. Zwingli's brand of Protestantism soon spread to many Swiss German villages.

A French Protestant named John Calvin, a theologian and author of a book called *Institutes of the Christian Religion*, also contributed to the Reformation in Switzerland. When Calvin came to Geneva, he claimed that the city was controlled by Satan. Determined to change the city's "evil" ways, Calvin soon gained a wide and powerful following that took control of the city and imposed very strict laws on the people.

Playing cards, wearing jewelry, and eating rich foods became punishable crimes. Everyone had to attend church twice on Sundays and be home by nine

The monument to the Reformation in Geneva is dedicated to four important figures from this historic period: (from left to right) *Guillaume Farel, John Calvin, Théodore de Bèze, and John Knox.*

every night. A group of ministers met on Thursdays to sentence the people who had broken these laws. Soon the city records were filled with minor offenses. One woman was put in jail for combing her hair improperly! Despite the efforts of Calvin and Zwingli, and many battles between Catholics and Protestants, Switzerland never became all Protestant. The two religious groups continued to fight for the next three centuries.

The French Takeover

In 1797, during one of the battles between the Catholics and the Protestants, the French dictator, Napoleon Bonaparte, saw his opportunity to move in and take control of new territories. Within six months, Napoleon had conquered the entire country. He destroyed the Swiss Confederation and set up the "Helvetian Republic."

The Swiss resented the strict laws enforced by Napoleon. They were used to the system under which each canton had its own set of laws. When Napoleon tried to form a single seat of government, a unified legal system, and a common monetary (money) system, the Swiss felt robbed of their independence.

The Swiss rebelled, and Napoleon's power soon began to weaken. He allowed Switzerland to become a Confederation of nineteen cantons. In 1815, Switzerland's full independence and permanent neutrality were guaranteed at the Congress of Vienna in Austria. Twelve years later, three more cantons joined the Confederation.

A New Constitution

Just as the government seemed to be taking shape, stability began to crumble once again. The Catholic cantons, desiring independence, broke off to form a separate government called the *Sonderbund*. Two years later, in 1847, a civil war erupted between seven Catholic cantons and the other Swiss cantons. Soon, the Catholics lost, the Sonderbund was dissolved, and Switzerland's warring years ended.

After the Sonderbund War, the Confederation could see that Switzerland needed a government with more central power. In 1848, the cantons' officials met and wrote a new constitution which increased the power of the central government and introduced a bicameral, or two-house, government. The new constitution recognized the equality of all Swiss citizens. It also guaranteed freedom of the press and freedom of worship, except for Jews who were included in this guarantee in 1866. The Constitution of 1848, with some minor changes, is still used today in Switzerland.

4. *The International Nation*

The years of peace following 1848 finally enabled Switzerland to become a country with more unified goals and interests. Switzerland was now in a position to help countries in need of protection.

The International Red Cross

For centuries, the Swiss were regarded as heroic but merciless fighters who slaughtered the enemy and left no survivors. After the Sonderbund War, however, the Swiss began to care about the wounded soldiers from other European nations in wartime.

In 1862, a journalist from Geneva named Jean-Henri Dunant helped organize a meeting of thirty-six people from fourteen countries in what was the beginning of the International Red Cross. The other countries at the meeting paid tribute to Switzerland by adopting as an emblem a red cross on a white background—the Swiss flag in reverse.

Today, the Red Cross participates in wartime and peacetime activities. The League of Red Cross Societies has its headquarters in Geneva, where Red Cross representatives from all over the world meet to discuss medi-

Jean-Henri Dunant helped start the International Red Cross.

cal and health care programs. The International Committee of the Red Cross, a neutral protector of victims during conflicts, works to ensure humane treatment of prisoners of war.

The Great War

Switzerland continued to work for peace. When World War I broke out in Europe, Switzerland promptly declared its neutrality on August 4, 1914. The war was sparked by the assassination of the heir to the throne of Austria-Hungary, Archduke Francis Ferdinand. Austria-Hungary, believing that Serbia was to blame, declared war. Other countries soon entered the conflict.

Germany thought that since so many Swiss spoke German, Switzerland should support the Central Powers (Germany and Austria-Hungary) against the Allies (France, Great Britain, and Russia). Switzerland strongly disagreed and chose to stay out of the fighting. Although no battles were fought on Swiss soil, the land-locked country could not help becoming somewhat involved in the war.

During World War I, Switzerland gave shelter to seventy thousand sick and wounded people from both sides, and continued to trade with all the surrounding countries. The Swiss exported dairy cows, which meant that milk had to be rationed. They did everything they could to make the most of their limited supplies. They even changed all of Switzerland's trains from coal-burning to electric ones.

The war finally ended on November 11, 1918, when the Germans accepted the armistice (truce) terms demanded by the Allied forces. The war devastated Europe. Ten million soldiers died, and twenty-one million were wounded in the war. At the Paris Peace Conference early in 1919, the Allied Powers and Germany signed the Treaty of Versailles.

The International Nation

The League of Nations

The League of Nations, headquartered at the Palace of Nations in Geneva, was formed after World War I to help prevent another world war. Switzerland joined the League on the condition that it would not be called upon to pick sides and fight in any future war, or allow fighting to occur on Swiss soil. In return for recognizing its neutrality, Switzerland agreed to cooperate with the group on economic and financial measures. Although the League's intentions were good, its organization was weak and ineffective. The League of Nations had not yet resolved its problems when another war erupted.

World War II

When World War II began, European countries were still recovering from the destruction of World War I. Powerful dictators in Germany, Italy, and the Soviet Union were ready to conquer the weakened countries. Adolf Hitler, the Nazi leader of the Third Reich, had his eye on neutral Switzerland—he even published maps showing Switzerland as a part of Germany.

Switzerland was quick to declare its neutrality and equally quick to build up its military defenses. Soon, the Swiss had mobilized 850,000 men. They threatened to blow up passes and tunnels to prevent the German soldiers from traveling across the country. Germany, afraid of cutting off its supply link to Italy, did not attack Switzerland. World War II finally ended when Germany surrendered to the Allies on May 7, 1945. Switzerland remained unharmed, but millions were killed on the European battlefields.

The United Nations

In another attempt to prevent future wars, a number of countries established the United Nations in 1945. This organization, much stronger than the League of Nations, was set up to work for peace and security. The United Nations tries to resolve problems between two or more countries before they turn to war. But if a war develops, the organization may be asked to help stop the fighting.

Because of Switzerland's policy of neutrality, it did not join the United Nations. Still, the Swiss showed their approval by establishing the European headquarters of the United Nations in Geneva. Switzerland became a member of many international organizations including UNESCO (the United Nations Educational, Scientific, and Cultural Organization), the International Labor Organization, the Council of Europe, the European Trade Association, and others.

The European headquarters for the United Nations is located in Geneva.

Switzerland is also a host to international negotiations. The United States and the Soviet Union held their Strategic Arms Limitations talks (SALT I and SALT II) in Geneva in the 1970s. More recently, in 1985, Geneva hosted the first Gorbachev-Reagan Summit and nuclear arms talks.

In Self-Defense

Although Switzerland's dedication to neutrality has held firm, the Swiss still fear the possibility of becoming involved in someone else's war. To defend themselves against possible attack, they have developed a strong military.

Every Swiss man who can must serve in the Swiss army, reporting for duty three weeks a year from the time he is twenty until he is fifty years old. Although some Swiss object to military service, others enjoy it. For them, it is an opportunity to spend time with old friends, and take a break from the usual routine of job and family.

The beautiful mountains of Switzerland are heavily fortified with miles of underground shelters and caverns filled with weapons. The military sites are well-disguised—many of them cut into hundreds of feet of solid rock. A common-looking barn opens up as an entrance to a large military arsenal. In one mountain forest, a large false tree stump covers the barrels of large guns emerging from an underground bunker. If a war does threaten Switzerland, the country will be ready.

Pollution Problems

Modern Switzerland has concerned itself with more than preserving peace and security. Its natural beauty is being destroyed daily by pollutants. Because Switzerland is located in central Europe, it receives more pollution from outside its borders than any other European

Acid rain has seriously damaged more than half the trees in the beautiful mountainous areas of southern Switzerland.

nation. Acid rain is now one of Switzerland's biggest problems. It is caused by gases in the smoke released by factories, trucks, cars, or any other machine that burns fossil fuels. Chemicals in the smoke combine with oxygen and water to form sulfuric and nitric acids. When these acids fall in rain, snow, or fog, they soak into the soil and run into rivers and lakes.

Eventually, the rain damages or kills plants and trees, and sometimes wildlife. In areas near industrial centers, 80 percent of the trees are gone. More than half of the trees in southern Switzerland are seriously damaged. If there are no trees to hold down the soil, erosion occurs. Usable land is so precious that the Swiss do not want to lose even the smallest piece of it.

The Swiss government is enforcing stricter air pollution laws for the factories, and is trying to persuade surrounding countries to do the same. Sixty percent of the Swiss own cars, which are the largest source of pollutants. People come to enjoy the mountains from all over Europe, and cars line up for several miles at the Swiss border during the summer months. Some Swiss think it would help to ban all cars on the roads on weekends. Yet Switzerland's economy relies heavily on tourist trade, so the government does not want to risk that success by allowing fewer people to visit Switzerland. There are no easy solutions to the problem of air pollution.

Industrial accidents also trouble the Swiss. Switzerland has several nuclear power plants and is planning to build more. When a nuclear power plant accident occurred at Chernobyl in the Soviet Union on May 26, 1986, it was a grim reminder to the world of how dangerous nuclear power can be. The disaster raised some serious questions about the safety of nuclear power plants.

After much discussion, an advisory board decided that Swiss safety rules were so strict that an incident such as Chernobyl would not be possible in Switzerland. Also, the board determined that nuclear energy was necessary to Swiss industry, and therefore to the economy. The issue continues to be debated.

Pollution in the Rhine River is another problem for the Swiss. In 1986, a large chemical fire in the Sandoz warehouse was extinguished with water that then drained into the Rhine. Streaming into the river with the water were poisonous herbicides, insecticides, and mercury. This accident killed plants, fish, and other wildlife for hundreds of miles along the Rhine, from Switzerland to Germany and beyond. Chemical spills continue to be the Rhine's greatest threat.

Switzerland is working to cope with new problems that come with a modern, industrialized world. Although Switzerland is a peaceful country, it is well prepared to defend itself against any internal or external forces that threaten it. When people think of Switzerland, many think of discipline, efficiency, and most of all, security. The Swiss want to keep it that way.

5. William Tell and Other Tales

The Swiss have many folktales and legends that the older people enjoy sharing with the young people. These stories are passed from generation to generation.

William Tell

The famous legend of William Tell came from the time when the Swiss rebelled against the powerful Habsburg family in the thirteenth century. To this day, Tell is remembered as one of the bravest fighters for Switzerland's freedom.

Tell was a large, strong man who lived on a mountainside near Altdorf by Lake Lucerne. He was known for his excellent aim with the crossbow, as well as for his bravery. He hated the ruling Habsburg governors, especially his local governor, Gessler, who was always thinking of new ways to torment the peasants and get more of their money. If they did not do exactly as he commanded, they were either killed or thrown into a dark dungeon for the rest of their lives.

One day a group of Gessler's soldiers came marching into Altdorf carrying a long thin pole. Several of the soldiers drove the pole deep into the hard brown dirt of

William Tell and Other Tales 61

the marketplace square, and placed a hat with a green peacock feather on the pole. One soldier announced that everyone over the age of twenty-one who passed the hat must kneel before it, as they would before Gessler or the emperor. Anyone who disobeyed would be thrown into prison. Two armed guards stood on either side of the pole to make sure the citizens carried out the command.

The next day William Tell and his young son strolled across the marketplace, deliberately ignoring the hat. The guards grabbed Tell and said, "You have disobeyed the governor's command. You must go to prison for the rest of your life."

Tell's heart burned deep within his chest. Grabbing the soldiers' swords as if they were small sticks, he threw them aside yelling, "I will kneel before my God, or the emperor, but never before an empty hat."

Before the guards could grab their swords again, Gessler, perched high atop his white steed, galloped into the market square. The guards rushed to tell him of Tell's disobedience. The cruel governor saw his chance for revenge. He noticed that Tell was carrying his crossbow, an act which was against the law. With a sneer, Gessler ordered the guards to seize Tell's son, stand him under a linden tree, and put an apple on the boy's head. Then Gessler commanded Tell to step back eighty paces from his son and shoot the apple off his head. If he were

SO LANG DIE BERGE
STEHN AUF IHREM
GRUNDE

successful, said the governor, Tell would be a free man.

A hush settled over the crowd as Tell slowly stepped off the eighty paces. He knelt and asked God to help him. Then rising, he took two arrows from his quiver. One he stuck in his belt, and the other he carefully slipped into his crossbow. He took aim and shot the arrow. As he split the apple exactly in half, the crowd cheered.

Gessler complimented Tell on his marksmanship, but wanted to know what the other arrow was for.

"If I had killed my child, your breast would have been the next target!" he cried.

Furious, Gessler ordered his guards to seize Tell, take him across the lake, and throw him in a dungeon, never to see daylight again.

Tell left his son in the care of his grandfather. As the guards forced Tell into a waiting boat, he called back, "Do not worry. God will watch over you."

After he was tightly chained in the boat, they started rowing toward the dungeon, which was across Lake Lucerne. Soon a terrible storm broke from the black clouds, and the waves tossed the boat about like a cork. Needing Tell to help row, the guards untied him. Tell grabbed the oars. With great strength, he steered the boat to a flat rock on the shore where they planned to wait until the storm passed. Before anyone could see what was happening, Tell grabbed his bow, turned the

The statue of William Tell and his son at Altdorf.

boat around, and jumped safely to shore. A great wave caught the boat, forcing it back to open water.

Tell walked to the nearest village where he heard that the guards had survived the storm. Walking to the dungeon, he hid in some nearby bushes to wait for Gessler. When he saw him coming up the narrow path, Tell placed another arrow in his bow and took aim. With one shot, he killed Gessler.

Tell escaped before anyone could catch him. When he returned to Altdorf, his friends met him with shouts of joy. Tell's daring deed was a signal to the other cantons around the lake to begin their fight for freedom.

Today, in the center of the market square in Altdorf, stands a statue of William Tell with one hand on his son and the other holding his crossbow. The famous German writer Friedrich Von Schiller wrote a play about William Tell, and Italian composer Gioacchino Rossini wrote an opera in 1829 about this folk hero. Whether or not William Tell really lived, he has become a Swiss symbol for freedom.

Charlemagne and the Snake

A legend about the emperor Charlemagne survives from the time of Switzerland's great wars. Because he was a wise and fair ruler, Charlemagne wanted all his subjects, even the poorest and humblest, to come to him with their troubles. He told his people to ring the bell outside of his door, and justice would be done.

One day Charlemagne heard the bell ringing softly. He sent two of his servants to see who it was. When they could find no one, the emperor went to look for himself. He saw a snake wrapped around the rope, looking at him with begging eyes. It then dropped to the ground and slid down a hill, constantly looking back to see if the emperor were following.

The kind emperor followed the snake. At last they came to the lakeshore where the snake had its nest. A hideous toad was sitting on the nest. Since the snake could not remove the toad without harming its eggs, Charlemagne immediately disposed of the toad.

After the eggs hatched, the snake appeared at Charlemagne's banquet table. It slid up to where his drinking cup was and dropped in a sparkling jewel. The emperor thanked the snake and had the gem set in gold. He presented it to his wife, who cherished the precious stone for the rest of her life.

The Blümlis Alp

Many of Switzerland's legends and folktales are about the mountains, good conquering evil, and events that happened during its struggle to become a confederation. Several of the folktales, however, try to explain some of the mysteries of the glaciers, the large bodies of ice and snow that move down the mountains or through the valleys.

A rich farmer and his wife from the canton of Bern were very happy, except that they wanted a child more than anything in the world. When they finally had a son, they spoiled him by giving him everything he wanted. Nothing was too good for him. They even bathed him in the finest cream. Sadly, the boy grew up to be mean and rude and caused his father to die of grief before his time.

The son inherited his father's house, barns, fields, and mountain pastures and became the herdsman and the head of the household. His favorite mountain pasture was the Blümlis Alp, or the Little Flower Alp, and during the summer, he went up there with his cattle. He left his mother to go hungry in the valley, while he gave his sweetheart, Katheryn, anything she wanted. After a while, he asked Katheryn to join him on the Alp, but she didn't want to walk over the stony paths with her new shoes. So the young herdsman tried to smooth the paths with butter. To make her climb easier, he built a stairway of cheese for her. When the work was finished, he hurried down the stairs to greet her. While the two lovers were together on the Alp, they laughed and played, thinking of no one but themselves.

The Blümlis Alp, or Little Flower Alp, is the setting for a well-known Swiss folktale.

Down in the valley, the young herdsman's mother was starving to death. Finally, hunger drove her to climb the mountain and beg for food. Her son gave her garbage to eat and sour milk to drink. The mother turned away and walked to the top of a nearby hill. She raised her hands and shouted to the heavens, "Mountains and rocks, fall down upon these sinners." Her words had not yet died away when the sky became as black as night. As lightning flashed, high winds battered her son's hut. The glacier above broke loose and slid down the mountain, burying everything in its path.

The Blümlis Alp still stands tall in the Bernese Oberland, covered with snow and glaciers. The surrounding pastures have so many tiny brightly colored alpine flowers that they look like one enormous blossom. But on dark stormy nights some say that the herdsman's cries can still be heard:

>I, my dog, my cow, and my fair bride
>Must stay forever on the Blümlis mountainside.

The Devil's Bridge

Another favorite Swiss folktale is about a high arched bridge over the Reuss River near the village of Goschenen. A long time ago, the people who lived there wanted to build a bridge over the wild and foaming river where it flows through a deep ravine. In those days there were no engineers, so no one knew how to construct it.

One day the Devil appeared before the city council and told them he would build the bridge. In return, the first person to cross the bridge was to be delivered body and soul to him. The council knew that dealing with the Devil was dangerous, but they needed the bridge so much that they agreed to his terms.

The next day, the bridge had been built. At the other end of it, the Devil sat waiting for his wages. Now that they had the bridge, the city council members did not want to keep their word. The chief of the council, who had been holding a goat, kicked it across the bridge with great force. Since the goat was the first living creature to cross the bridge, the Devil had to be content with his reward.

Morning Has Gold in Its Mouth

The Swiss have many folk sayings and proverbs. Here is a Swiss German one that the children like to write on their classroom blackboard for the teacher to read:

Der Himmel ist blau
Das Wetter ist schön

Herr Lehrer, wir wollen
spazieren gehen.

(The sky is blue
The weather is beautiful
Mr. Teacher, we would like
To go for a walk.)

Another proverb stemming from German tradition is *"Morgen Stund hat Gold im Mund,"* or "Morning has gold in its mouth." The English version of this is "The early bird gets the worm," meaning that the morning hours are best to get the most accomplished.

When a person is quiet, but thinking, Swiss Germans would say, *"Stille Wasser sind tiefe Wasser,"* or "Still waters run deep."

A few sayings predict the weather. Almost every Swiss German knows this one about the Niesen mountain:

Hat der Niesen einen Hut, Ist das Wetter gut.
Hat er einen Kragen darf man es wagen.
Hat er einen Degen, bleibt zuhaus es gibt Regen.

(When the Niesen has a hat, the weather will be good.
If it wears a collar, one can take a chance.
If it has a dagger, stay home; it will rain.)

The French- and Italian-speaking Swiss also have

their own proverbs. The French Swiss might say: "*Dis-moi ce que tu manges, je te dirai ce que tu es*," or "Tell me what you eat, I will tell you who you are." The Italian Swiss might say, "*Se non e vero, e ben travato*," or "If it is not true, it is well made up."

    The Swiss treasure their legends, folktales, and sayings. These stories and bits of folk wisdom are an important part of their national heritage.

6. Celebrating Swiss Style

Switzerland, a nation of many traditions, celebrates its heritage with holidays and festivals of all kinds. The hard-working Swiss enjoy time spent with friends and family during holidays. Except for Swiss National Day, the celebrations vary from canton to canton, and often reflect local traditions.

Swiss National Day

All parts of Switzerland celebrate National Day on August 1. On this day in 1291, the cantons of Uri, Schwyz, and Unterwalden met to form an alliance which started the Swiss Confederation. This national holiday is celebrated with speeches, folk dancing, and parades in which men, women, and children wear native costumes. Cantonal and national flags decorate all the buildings and streets. Parties, fireworks, bell-ringing, and beacon fires in the mountains contribute to the festivities. The beacon fires are a reminder of the days when fires were used as signals between different mountain towns. Because the Swiss take such pride in their independence, National Day is the festival they treasure the most.

The Unspunnen Festival in Interlaken.

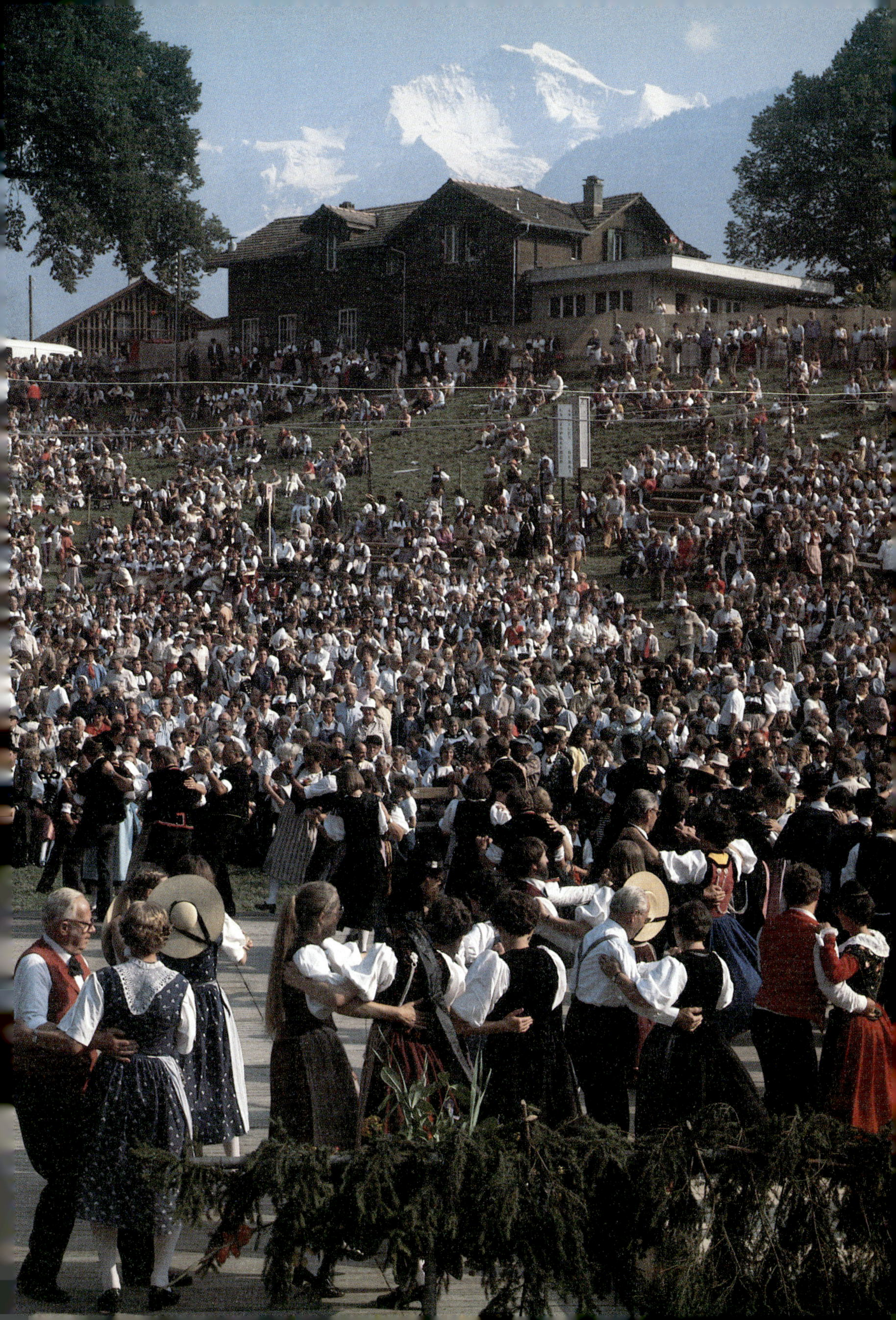

A Swiss Christmas

Most Swiss are Christians, and Catholics and Protestants alike celebrate Christmas in a variety of ways. Switzerland's four ways of saying Christmas are: *Weihnachten* (German), *Noël* (French), *Natale* (Italian), and *Nadel* (Romansh).

The Christmas season starts with Advent, which is usually the first Sunday in December. On that day, children begin to open the doors of their Advent calendar, a Christmas picture with numbered doors that mark the days until Christmas. Although these calendars can be purchased in stores, many children make theirs in school. In some Catholic regions of Switzerland, children spend time before Christmas preparing a *crèche*, or cradle, and a stall to represent Jesus' birthplace in Bethlehem. These Nativity scenes are often placed under their trees on Christmas Day.

The Christmas festivities officially begin on December 6. For many Swiss, that is *Samiklaus Abend*, or Santa Claus Night. A neighbor disguised in a beard and in a black, white, or red costume appears after the family supper. *Samiklaus* comes to find out if the children have been bad or good. He is loved and feared because he carries not only a burlap bag of candies and nuts, but also a bundle of willow branches. Samiklaus gives each child a playful tap with the willow switch in

The children's fairyland special on the Bahnhofstrasse.

case the child has been naughty during the year. After that, he passes out his treats and listens to each child's Christmas wishes. He then tells Christkindli (Christ Child) what the child wants, and Christkindli comes bearing gifts on Christmas Eve.

In some places, Christkindli makes the village rounds in a sleigh drawn by six reindeer. He carries a load of toys and other gifts, and Christmas trees decorated with apples, oranges, nuts, and cookies. But in the village of Halwill, Christkindli is a girl dressed in white, who wears a sparkling crown on her head. She is accompanied by children dressed in white robes who carry lighted lanterns and baskets of gifts.

In many Swiss homes, the Christmas tree is decorated secretly behind closed doors on December 24. The doors stay shut until after the Christmas Eve supper is served. Supper usually consists of tasty breads, sausages, and cookies. After the meal, the doors are flung open. The children and adults gather around the tree to light the candles, sing carols, and open the gifts. Since the Swiss are a practical people, most of the gifts are sensible items such as household goods or warm hats, mittens, socks, and jackets. After the families celebrate their own Christmas, many go to church at midnight. Church bells ring across the valleys before the ceremonies begin, signaling the beginning of a day celebrated by Swiss Christians.

A Swiss church decorated for Christmas.

Fastnacht Carnival

In the late winter, one of Switzerland's most colorful and dramatic festivals is the Fastnacht Carnival in Basel. This carnival is similar to the Mardi Gras festival in New Orleans, Louisiana. It occurs on the three days before Ash Wednesday, the beginning of Lent. The festival opens in the market square at four o'clock in the

During the Fastnacht Carnival in Basel, men dressed in colorful costumes and masks march through the streets.

morning. Men dress in bright costumes and wear huge, strange-looking masks. Some of the costumes are designed to poke fun at local politicians.

The men with piccolos and drums march through the streets making as much noise as possible, and star drummers give concerts along the way. When the street lights come on at 5:00 A.M., everyone hurries to a favo-

Celebrating Swiss Style 79

rite restaurant for a hot bowl of *Mehlsuppe,* or brown flour soup. The parade begins again in the evenings, with the marchers carrying bright lanterns to light their way. Every night after the parade is a masked ball.

Other carnivals are celebrated throughout Switzerland before Lent. In Flums, men parade through the streets wearing wooden masks, which are handed down from father to son. Some of the masks are more than a hundred years old. At Einsiedeln, the "Carnival Runners" wear scary masks, and carry huge, clanging bells on their backs. The bells are so heavy that the men cannot stand up straight. The masks and noise are supposed to drive out the cold winter, and the clanging of bells rings in the warm spring.

Easter Celebrations

On Easter, many Swiss families attend church, where they will hear the Easter story from the Bible and listen to special Easter music. After church, the Swiss spend the rest of the day enjoying themselves with Easter egg hunts and other activities. Boys and girls also receive chocolate Easter bunnies and chocolate eggs as treats, and adults exchange chocolate treats.

Pfingsten (Feast of the Pentecost) is a religious holiday that takes place on the seventh Sunday after Easter. Candlelight processions and parades are often

A Swiss boy in Zurich looks at eggs decorated for the Easter celebration.

held on this occasion. The Monday after Pfingsten is also a holiday for the Swiss.

On the first Thursday after Pentecost, the cantons that are mostly Catholic celebrate Corpus Christi (Body of Christ). It is a festival of rejoicing, and many of the ceremonies date back to the fourteenth and fifteenth centuries. The church altars are decorated with green branches and garlands of flowers. In parades, men dress in old army uniforms, and women dress in traditional local costumes. These beautiful dresses are handed down from the mother to the oldest daughter. The other daughters have to buy a new dress if they want one. Since many of the dresses are decorated with sterling silver chains, they now cost several thousand dollars. Not every Swiss woman owns one, and if she does, she takes great pride in it.

Sechseläuten

Another big festival is the two-day *Sechseläuten*, or the "six o'clock ringing." This festival, held in Zurich during the second or third week of April, dates back to the fourteenth century when the city's trade or craft workers rebelled against the rich nobles and merchants. They formed guilds, or workers' clubs, which controlled Zurich's government until the French Revolution at the end of the eighteenth century.

During the Sechseläuten *festival in Zurich, members of the city's twenty-four guilds take part in parades.*

Today, the guilds have changed from political organizations to exclusive men's clubs, and it is very difficult to join one. Some guilds accept only sons of members. One man offered a million francs to join, and he was still refused membership.

Members of the twenty-four guilds parade proudly through the streets wearing elaborate costumes. Some of them look like American colonial military uniforms. Each guild also has its own emblem. For example, the tailor's guild carries big scissors. When its members parade through the streets, they cut women's silk

The burning of the **Böögg**.

scarves, ribbons, and men's ties. Members of the boatmen's guild carry baskets of fish that they throw into the crowds. Women often greet passing marchers with flowers and a kiss.

The highlight of the festival is the burning of the *Böögg*, or bogeyman, at six o'clock on the second day. The Böögg is a large snowman made out of cotton that is perched on a pile of scrapwood, soaked with gas, and stuffed with explosives. The well-timed parade ends a few minutes before six on Bellevue Square, where the Böögg is mounted. As the sixth bell rings from Saint

Peter's Church, the snowman is set on fire. While it is burning, church bells ring, fifes and drums play, men on horseback ride around the square, and people sing and dance. In about fifteen minutes, the ceremony is over, and everyone leaves for a night of banquets and parties.

Local Festivals

In late spring and early summer, some of the small mountain villages have festivals celebrating the time when the young cows are driven to the mountain pastures. For this, people decorate their cows' necks with neck straps embroidered with brightly colored designs and huge bells. A small tree or bouquets of flowers are fastened between the cow's horns. The men who drive the cattle to the high pastures return only a few times before fall, for supplies of food.

Summertime is filled with more local festivals. There are international music festivals in Montreux, Lucerne, and Gstaad. The William Tell Festival begins in June in Interlaken. There, Schiller's play about William Tell is performed several times a week until the summer tourist season ends.

The fall season is almost as busy. Morgarten celebrates the first Confederation Victory in November. Before that, there are numerous harvest festivals. One of the most colorful is the onion festival in Bern. Garlands

Celebrating Swiss Style 85

of onions hang everywhere, and strands of onion braids fill the market square.

Switzerland's holidays and festivals mark the celebration of hundreds of years of Swiss tradition. Such festive occasions are times for the Swiss to relax and enjoy food, family, and friends.

7. Chalets, Cheese, and Chocolate

"Wie die Alten sungen, so zwitschern auch die Jungen" is a Swiss German saying which translates into "As the old ones sing, so chirp the young ones." This means the young will copy the older people. Swiss parents work hard to set a good example for their children. "The family comes first," is something all Swiss will tell you. Family ties are so strong that each family is like a mini-community.

Parents want their children to respect their elders. Swiss German parents might tell them, *"Ehre das Alter"* which means "honor old age." They also teach the children to work before they go to school. The young ones clear dishes off the table and help pick up their toys and clothes. As the children grow older, their responsibilities increase. The girls often learn how to cook, sew, and knit when they are eight years old. They are also expected to help with the dishes and cleaning. However, the girls don't like it if the boys don't have to work as hard as they do.

Most of the boys do work just as hard as the girls. Although they have little to do with household chores, they run errands for their parents, and attend to other tasks. Before families had cars, the boys had to clean

Throughout Switzerland, people grow fresh fruits and vegetables in the small plots called Schrebergarten.

and oil the family bicycles. Since many of the older homes were heated with wood, the boys had to help cut and stack wood, and keep the wood box filled in cold weather. Most families have a small garden, and the boys help the fathers weed, hoe, and water it with sprinkling cans.

The Swiss love to garden. Even in the big cities, they can grow their fresh vegetables and fruits in small plots called *Schrebergarten*. About a hundred years ago, a German doctor named Daniel Schreber urged city authorities to set aside land that could be used for gardening. There people could escape the urban stress by digging in the earth and growing some of their own food. The idea caught on. Today there are Schrebergartens throughout Germany, Austria, and Switzerland. Because people rent these large spaces for twenty years or more, they build small huts that are used for tool sheds or just a place to have lunch and play a few games of Jass with friends.

Most people in Switzerland have a high standard of living, and most live in the city. The Swiss are moving to urban areas in larger numbers, in search of new opportunities that the cities offer. Since property is expensive and scarce in the small nation, most urban families live in apartment buildings.

Families who have the good fortune to own a house take great pride in it. They often decorate the windowsills with brightly colored flowers. Like everything else in Switzerland, the architectural styles vary from canton to canton.

A house in the Bernese Oberland near the mountain region has a low, pitched roof with wide eaves on all sides. Such a house is called a *Schali*, or chalet. Tall, sun-browned wooden houses in the Valais area of southwestern Switzerland are built on a whitewashed masonry base that rests on wooden stilts with large flat stones at the top. Elevating the structure above the ground helps keep out rats, mice, and other rodents.

This Bernese farm house has living quarters and a barn.

Many of these houses can be seen in Zermatt, a town near the steep, snowy slopes of the Matterhorn.

The houses of the Engadine in eastern Switzerland are different from other Swiss houses. The inside is built of wood, but the outside is covered with a light-colored hard plaster called stucco. The stucco is covered with sgraffito decorations. These might be floral or geometric designs, but sometimes they are pictures of animals or historical scenes.

In the Ticino area of southern Switzerland, the houses are built from rough stone. Even the roofs are

Geometric designs decorate this house in the Engadine.

made from stone slabs. There are balconies where the women often dry fruit and vegetables, cook *polenta* (cornmeal), and roast chestnuts. Now many of the older houses are used as vacation homes.

Newer houses do not differ as much from canton to canton as the older ones do. Many of them are one-family dwellings and look similar to new houses in the United States. Yet they cost about three times more than American houses.

Swiss homes are usually comfortable and have a friendly atmosphere. The rooms are well organized. Many of the closets, shelves, and drawers are built into the walls. Of all the rooms in the house, Swiss kitchens are designed to be the most efficient. Most have built-in storage shelves and wall closets with pull-out drawers for blenders, meat and bread cutters, coffee grinders, beaters, and many other appliances. Since the Swiss may spend hours each day planning and preparing meals, the kitchen is one of the most important rooms in the house.

Food, Glorious Food

Swiss families often eat all three daily meals together. Breakfast consists of coffee with hot milk and sugar, bread, butter, cheese, and jam. Some families, particularly farm families, serve a very strong hot coffee with an equal amount of milk in a large bowl. People "eat" the coffee like soup with a piece of firm bread. However, guests are usually served coffee in a regular cup with bread, butter, and jam on the side.

Another popular Swiss breakfast is *Birchermüsli*, which is sometimes even served for lunch or dinner. Dr. Bircher-Brenner introduced it in his health clinic around the turn of the century as the "fruit diet." He believed that fresh fruits and nuts were healthier than the rich, starchy diets of his time. Birchermüsli is an easy breakfast to make, especially using the following recipe.

Birchermüsli
(One serving)

1/2 cup of quick-cooking oatmeal (uncooked)
1 cup of chopped fruit—any kind can be used, even bananas
2 tablespoons chopped nuts or wheat germ
3/4 to 1 cup milk
1/2 cup yogurt (optional)
Combine all ingredients and serve immediately.

The Swiss may also serve their guests a large braided egg bread called *Eierzopf* for breakfast or for special occasions. When a local grocery store was celebrating

These guests in a Swiss house enjoy a special braided bread, Eierzopf, *for breakfast.*

the anniversary of its opening, the owners gave customers pieces of Eierzopf cut from a fifty-foot (fifteen-meter) loaf that was decorated with red ribbons. By five o'clock in the afternoon, only crumbs were left.

Because lunchtime lasts for two hours, most Swiss go home at midday, and stores, businesses, and schools close during this time. For the Swiss, this is the big meal of the day. Both the midday and evening meals start with soup. Soup was once the staple of Swiss life, and large pots of soup were cooked for hours on a back burner. Today, many Swiss use an easier method. Switzerland is the country that invented packaged dry soups. Grocers sell the Swiss Maggi and Knorr soups all over the world, since they are tasty and easy to prepare from the directions on the box.

The main part of the midday meal consists of meatballs, spaghetti, or some kind of sausage served with *Rösti* (fried potatoes similar to hash browns), and several kinds of vegetables or salad. Rösti is a favorite potato dish in the German part of Switzerland, and is usually eaten at least once a day.

Kartoffelrösti (Fried Potato Cake)
(About four servings)

2 pounds of unpeeled potatoes
4 tablespoons butter
3/4 teaspoon salt
2 tablespoons hot water

Boil the potatoes with their skins, and cool. (It is best to cook them a day ahead.) When they are completely cooled, peel and grate them into coarse shreds. Heat the butter in a large skillet. Gradually add the potatoes and salt. Cook over low heat, turning frequently with a spatula until the potatoes are soft and yellow. Press the potatoes with the spatula into a flat cake. Sprinkle with hot water.

Chalets, Cheese, and Chocolate

Cover and cook over low heat 15 to 20 minutes or until they are crusty and golden at the bottom. Turn the potatoes into a hot serving dish crusty side up and serve immediately.

Adults might drink a glass of wine with their noonday meal, while the children drink cider or some other kind of fruit juice. The Swiss do not drink as much milk as Americans do. They do not drink much water, either, and have difficulty understanding why anyone would. Drinks are usually served hot or at room temperature.

If any leftovers remain from the noon meal, the Swiss warm them up for supper. Even unfinished bread might be saved for later. A Swiss supper is a light, simple meal. One quick and easy supper dish is *Omeletten*, an egg pancake, sometimes served with canned or fresh fruit over the top. Another light supper is bread and butter, jam, a piece of cheese or sausage, coffee or herb tea, and perhaps a glass of beer to top off the meal.

Swiss Cheese

Because the Swiss have so many dairy cows, wonderful cheeses are a Swiss trademark. Most rural villages have a small dairy. A farmer milks his cows, puts the milk into large cans, loads them onto a tractor or a

An experienced Swiss cheesemaker cuts and breaks coagulated milk into small pieces with a harplike instrument.

horse-drawn wagon, and drives the milk directly to the dairy. At the dairy, people weigh the milk and give the farmer credit for that amount. Once a week they add up the farmer's account and pay it. While fathers often teach their children the art of cheesemaking, becoming a certified cheesemaker takes a ten-year apprenticeship and a week of exams.

Young people enjoy a fondue *by dipping a long fork with a bite-sized piece of bread into the cheese and wine mixture.*

Emmentaler and Gruyère are the two best-known Swiss cheeses. Emmentaler is made in the German part of Switzerland, and Gruyère in the French part. Although the two cheeses are hard to tell apart, Emmentaler has bigger holes and is softer and moister. This is what Americans call Swiss cheese.

One favorite Swiss cheese dish is *fondue*, which means "melted" in French. Most Swiss own a fondue set, a fireproof ceramic dish that is set on a rack over a small flame. The fondue is made from shredded Emmentaler and Gruyère cheese, dry white wine, and cherry brandy called Kirsch. The cheese mixture is melted over a high flame in a cooking dish in the center of the table. Then everyone spears a bite-sized piece of bread on a long-handled fork, dips it into the fondue, and puts the entire morsel in their mouths.

Another popular cheese dish, called *Raclette*, is made by melting cheese in front of a fire on a stove. The melted cheese is spread on boiled potatoes or hard bread, and is eaten with pickled onions.

Sweets for the Swiss

Because breakfast is served between 5:00 and 7:00 in the morning, a snack called *Znüni* is traditionally served around 9:00 A.M. Coffee with milk, cocoa, and some kind of coffeecake or a piece of chocolate are eaten then. Chocolate is a staple food for children, soldiers, and mountaineers.

The Swiss export more than fifteen million dollars worth of chocolate every year. Tobler and Lindt chocolates are available in the United States and elsewhere, but the Swiss are their own best customers. Tobler makes three hundred varieties for the Swiss alone, and every town has at least one chocolate shop.

One woman went to a supermarket where she counted eighty-seven different kinds of candy bars, and thirty-seven varieties of boxed chocolate candy. A

A man takes a bite of a doughnut-shaped loaf of Swiss bread.

Swiss who had been living in Michigan for twenty years returned to his homeland and bought so many chocolate bars to take back to the United States that he filled one small suitcase. He ate most of them himself.

Wonderful cakes, cookies, and other desserts highlight many Swiss holiday occasions. Professional bakers make the most elegant Swiss cakes. When a housewife wants to honor her family or guest, she will buy a special cake or torte at her favorite shop. Every town has a *Konditorei* or *confiserie* where people can buy delicious desserts and coffee, cocoa, or tea. At four in the afternoon, many Swiss women—and a few men—go to one of these shops for a delicious dessert.

Swiss women bake many kinds of cookies at home, especially during the Christmas season. One favorite kind is the *Kräbeli*, or aniseed cookies. The *Basler Leckerli* is a honey biscuit filled with candied fruit and nuts that Swiss people have been baking for more than five hundred years. In the canton of Valais, *Ringli*, or doughnutlike cakes, are served on Christmas Eve with hot chocolate.

Zurich's *Tirggel* is made from flour and honey, and is thin, hard, and shiny. The dough used to be pressed into molds shaped like cows, sheep, or pigs, but today many of the molds are cartoon and storybook characters. Some of them are as large as windowpanes. Since the cakes stay fresh for months, people sometimes use them to decorate their homes.

From Birchermüsli to fondue, hearty Swiss meals rarely leave people hungry. Eating well, and eating for enjoyment, are important to the Swiss.

8. Education, the Swiss Way

Education is taken seriously in Switzerland, and almost all of the Swiss can read and write. The country has some of the finest schools in the world. Parents from many nations send their children to Switzerland's five hundred private schools. All Swiss young people are required to attend school for about nine years, and the public schools are free. Since each canton has a different school system, the schools are the responsibility of each canton's government.

Primary and secondary schools (grades one through nine) are required. In most cantons, primary school includes grades one through six. Secondary school usually has grades seven through nine. Unlike most American students, Swiss students go to school four full days and two half-days a week. They usually have Wednesday and Saturday afternoons free, but that varies from canton to canton. School days often begin at eight in the morning and end at four in the afternoon, with a two-hour lunch break. After school, the work does not stop; most students spend several hours studying or doing chores.

The Swiss grading system is also somewhat different from the usual American system. Grades are handed out twice a year, and range from one to four rather than A to F. A *one* is the best grade. Students are graded for effort, achievement, and behavior. These records are kept in a hard cover "grade book" which parents have to sign. If the grades are poor, a young person's life may not be pleasant for a while.

Swiss German students begin to learn high German as early as their first year in primary school. French- and Italian-speaking Swiss also learn German, but they begin their German studies later.

Languages are taught slowly, so that they never seem impossible to learn. The children must concentrate so hard in order to learn another language that many teachers have them sing several songs in between each lesson. The children also have two fifteen-minute recess periods to take a break from their studies.

By the time students reach the fifth grade, school becomes more difficult. Fifth grade in Switzerland is like seventh or eighth grade in the United States. Students begin their day with the more difficult classes. Geography is an important subject, and is often the class where students begin to imagine traveling abroad.

Sometimes students visit the places they have studied, or take a field trip. One springtime trip is a boat tour of Lake Geneva. If the boat passes a historic spot such as the Castle of Chillon, the teacher may gather the students around to tell them about it.

Swiss students on a field trip.

When students finish secondary school at age fifteen or sixteen, they may continue their studies at the Gymnasium. In Switzerland, a Gymnasium is similar to a high school in the United States, only much more difficult. One type of Gymnasium specializes in classical studies of Greek and Latin, another in Latin and modern languages, and a third in mathematics and science.

Most young people do not attend the Gymnasium. Instead, these students take a *Lehre*, or a two- to five-year apprenticeship which allows them to combine school with work in their chosen field. Only a small percentage of students in apprenticeships go on to college because they already have the job training they need.

The students who do decide to pursue a college education may attend one of the nine major universities in Switzerland. The oldest is the University of Basel, which was founded in 1459. About thirty thousand students attend Swiss universities, and about one-fifth of these students come from other countries.

Johann Heinrich Pestalozzi

Switzerland did not always have public education. For centuries, reading and writing were taught only to the rich and powerful upper classes. Even then, the schools were not very good by today's standards. Many teachers could not add and subtract, and the children learned only to read the Bible. Every year they would start at the beginning and read every word in the entire book. Children hated those lessons and did them only because they had to.

During the 1840s, the Swiss started a public school system, mainly because of the efforts of Johann Heinrich Pestalozzi (1746-1827). Until his time, nobody thought that poor children were capable or worthy of learning to read, write, and do arithmetic.

Johann Heinrich Pestalozzi and his son.

Pestalozzi wanted to educate the poor so they could get better jobs and raise their social status. He believed that they would learn if they were given love and a simple but regular life. He bought a small farm and began a school for the poor children. After the children settled into a routine, they learned well, proving his theories were correct. He also thought that the work the children did on the farm would support his program, but he was wrong. Eventually he had to sell some of his land to pay off debts, and he was forced to close his school.

For the next twenty years, he wrote books. His most famous book was *Leonard and Gertrude*, which was about social reform through education. His books received a gold medal from the Bern Economic Society, inscribed *Civi optimo* (for a most excellent citizen).

Pestalozzi was forced to close several of his schools throughout his life, but he devoted himself to researching the best teaching methods. He never gave up his dream that all children should have a secure home, love, and an education. Pestalozzi died in 1827, believing his methods were good. He also believed that he had failed to convince the Swiss of the worth of those methods. Little did he realize that one day Switzerland would have a public school system and that his techniques would be taught to teachers all over the world.

More than a hundred years later, Switzerland created a village for children who had lost their homes during World War II. On August 28, 1946, the cornerstone was laid for the *Kinderdorf Pestalozzi*. Today, a small village affectionately called *Pestalozzidorf* lies near Trogen in the canton of Appenzell. Only a few years after the village was started, the Swiss decided to open it to orphan children from all over the world, some from as far away as Tibet. The houses have international names such as Les Cigales, Jukola, Kukoricza, Yambhu Lagang, or Al-Amal, which indicate the nationality of the fifteen to twenty children who live in

Education, the Swiss Way

each house. Couples who are the same nationality as the children take the place of real parents as they try to create the feeling of a national family. They speak their native tongue and retain native customs. Pictures and wall hangings decorate the houses, reminding the children of their homeland. On their national holidays, their own flag is raised over the house.

When the young people are ready to graduate, they receive a document called a *Bürgerbrief*, or a miniature citizenship to the Children's Village. Accompanying it is a letter with the best wishes from the village and a statement expressing the hope that the young person will live up to the principles taught at Pestalozzi Village.

Nothing could be a more fitting monument to Pestalozzi than this village. It truly practices his dreams of education, and a chance in life for all young people.

9. The World's Playground

Many Swiss participate in sports, and one-third of the population belongs to one of Switzerland's sixty-eight sports organizations. Although the Swiss keep themselves physically fit, they do not emphasize the competitive aspect of sports as much as Americans do. Most Swiss will tell you that sports are just a hobby with them.

One sports organization is Youth and Sports, which is for young people between the ages of fourteen and twenty. Besides providing hours of enjoyment, these sports programs help prepare men for army duty.

The Swiss Rifle Association has more members than any sports organization. The men often join because they are required to meet a certain standard of shooting performance for the army. If they don't, they have to take additional courses until they improve. As a result of this thorough training, the Swiss are known as excellent marksmen.

Soccer, called *Fussball* (football), is very popular in Switzerland. The Swiss Soccer Association is one of the nation's largest sports organizations.

The Swiss refer to any physical exercises as gymnastics, and these programs begin when a child first

A family enjoys a Sunday hike near the Matterhorn.

starts school. The Federal Society of Gymnastics helps develop gymnastics teams in many cantons, and nearly every town has a team. When the team wins a major competition, the whole town celebrates by going to the train station to welcome the returning team.

Gymnastics are not just for the young. People of all ages participate for as long as they are able. Most retired people spend several hours a week exercising at a nearby gym. A few years ago, an eighty-seven-year-old woman won a medal in a gymnastics competition.

Schwingen, Unspunnen Stein, and Hornussen

Three sports that are played only in Switzerland are *Schwingen, Unspunnen Stein,* and *Hornussen.* Schwingen, or Swiss wrestling, is different from ordinary wrestling. The two opponents wear short leather, cotton, or linen shorts over their regular long pants. They are required to take hold of each other's trunks. While holding firmly to them, one wrestler must lift his opponent off the ground before he throws him. Swiss wrestling meets are held outside during the summer months and are often combined with other festivals. Sometimes more than 200 contestants attract as many as 3,500 spectators.

Unspunnen Stein, or stone putting, dates back to 1805 when the first stone-putting festival was held in the town of Unspunnen. In this sport, a player must lift a very heavy, egg-shaped stone as high as his head, and throw it as far as possible. Mostly big, heavy-set men participate in wrestling and stone putting, because these sports require tremendous strength.

Hornussen, played mainly in the Bernese Emmental, is often called "farmer's tennis," and it resembles American baseball. The "bats," which are boards mounted on long handles, are used to hit the *Hornuss,* which looks like a wooden hockey puck. In the field, the players catch the Hornuss with wooden rackets.

Two young men compete in a Swiss wrestling match at the Federal Wrestling and Alpine Herdsmen's Festival.

School Sports

Like many other things in Switzerland, a few sports are played in some cantons and not in others. _Schlagball_ is one of these. Children in Thurgau spend hours playing this game, while many children living in the canton of Saint Gallen, less than twenty-five miles (forty kilometers) away, do not play it. Schlagball is much like American softball except that there are four bases instead of three. There is no catcher or pitcher; the batter stands between first and fourth base, throws the ball up, and hits it.

A game that most Swiss children learn is *Völkerball*, which is similar to team dodge ball. The players form two equal teams, which face each other in a rectangular playing area. One team attempts to eliminate the players on the other team by hitting them with a ball about the size of a volleyball. The idea is to hit an opposing team member below the waist with the ball. Members of the other team, in turn, try to catch the ball and throw it back before it hits them. The team that hits the most players wins.

On Horseback

Many of the cantons have excellent riding schools for horseback riders. The small town of Maienfeld in eastern Switzerland has a riding school and a hotel where visitors can come with their horses. During the afternoon coffee hour, the horses stand patiently next to an outside table while their owners have some refreshments.

Christine Stückelberger is Switzerland's best rider in dressage, a technique where the rider and horse work

Either alone or in groups from one of Switzerland's excellent riding schools, many Swiss enjoy horseback riding as a way to experience the beauty of their nation's countryside.

together as one unit. She won the Olympic championship in 1976, and in 1986 won a silver medal in the world dressage competitions in Kansas. Dressage is difficult for the rider and the horse to learn; it can take years to train for the upper levels of competition.

Outdoor Adventures

The Swiss take advantage of their mountains and lakes for hours of outdoor fun. Many Swiss keep physically fit by hiking in the mountains almost every weekend. As soon as children are able to walk, their families take them on hikes. By the time they are in their twenties, they have developed strong legs and lungs. Many people over sixty years old can hike up trails at a rapid pace.

During the summer, some young people train for the five-day mountain run, which is held in the middle of August. To prepare for this event, they run up and down mountain trails as fast as they can for several hours. If you run up and down a hill a few times in a row, you will see how exhausting it is.

Every weekend Switzerland's back roads are filled with hundreds of bikers. Some are practicing for the Tour de Suisse, which is held in June. In 1986, 133 professional bikers from all over the world rode in the nine-day race, circling the country and covering almost 1,000 miles (1,610 kilometers). Each day the bikers go as far as 150 miles (240 kilometers) or as short a distance as 15 miles (24 kilometers) when they are in the mountains. Since most of Switzerland is hilly or mountainous, the Tour tests the strength and endurance of the athletes.

Boating is also popular with the Swiss, who skim over the surfaces of Switzerland's lakes on the weekends in small sailboats and windsurfers. Even sudden rainstorms don't discourage the boaters. Every summer, sailboats crowd Lake Geneva for the annual *Bol d' Or*, or Gold Cup, yacht race. In July the European and World Surfing Championships are held on Lake Sils near Silvaplana in the eastern part of Switzerland. This competition is such a popular event that it had to limit the number of competitors to five hundred.

Skis, Skates, and Sleds

The Swiss also enjoy winter sports, and they are proud that their small country hosted the 1928 and 1948 Winter Olympic Games. Nearly all the Swiss can ski well. In the mountain areas, children begin to ski almost as soon as they can walk. Their parents take great pride in teaching them.

Cross-country skiing is continually gaining in popularity. Every year more than 12,000 cross-country skiers compete in the Engadine Ski Marathon, which is a 26-mile (41.6-kilometer) run from Maloja to Auoz in southeastern Switzerland.

The Swiss often win medals for skiing, figure skating, and bobsledding in international competitions. Erika Hess, a skier, won a bronze medal in the 1980

A ski school for children in Switzerland.

Olympics at Lake Placid, New York. In 1981, she won every international slalom competition, including the World Cup. In 1984 and 1985, she won the World Cup again, as well as a gold medal at the World Alpine championships. Three Swiss skiers took home medals from the 1988 Winter Olympics in Calgary, Canada. Pirmin Zurbriggen won a gold and a bronze, Peter

Müller won a silver, and Vreni Schneider won two gold medals.

In 1981, Denise Biellman won the world's figure skating competition in Connecticut. She did a new spin that was so spectacular that it is now known as the Biellman Spin. In this maneuver, the skater spins on the left foot while holding the right up overhead. Not all figure skaters can perform this move, because it goes beyond a full split.

Whether they are hiking, boating, bicycling, or skiing, the Swiss enjoy a variety of sports and recreation. Their beautiful lakes and mountains offer many opportunities to get outside, play, and enjoy the natural wonders of the land.

10. To Begin Again

The Swiss have been coming to North America for a long time. Some people came to find political and business opportunities, while others came for adventure or as an escape from punishment. Most of them, however, came for land and for religious freedom.

One religious group settled in Pennsylvania in the late seventeenth century. This group, organized in Zurich, called themselves Mennonites after their leader, Menno Simmons. Later they divided into several other groups, including the Amish.

The members of these groups are pacifists, which means they are against war. Since that idea was totally unacceptable to the Dutch, German, and Swiss governments, the pacifists living in those countries were treated cruelly.

When William Penn, a Quaker from Pennsylvania, offered them the chance to come to America, they eagerly accepted. At last they would live in a land where they could believe what they liked and have freedom of religion. Many Swiss, such as Amish leader Joseph Schantz (1749-1813) and Mennonite leader Peter Lehmann (1776-1843), worked hard to establish and develop their religious communities in the New World.

The Amish drive horse-drawn carriages instead of modern vehicles such as cars and tractors.

Many of these Mennonite and Amish communities thrived, and still do today. Although Mennonites accept modern practices, such as driving cars and tractors, the Amish have resisted change. They have maintained a way of life that is much like life on a typical farm in Switzerland during the seventeenth and eighteenth centuries. They drive horse-drawn carriages and use only mules and horses to work their land. Amish barns have electricity to refrigerate the milk storage tanks, but they light their homes with kerosene lanterns and use wood-burning stoves for heat.

Typical Amish homes are simple: the windows have muslin curtains, the shiny wooden floors are bare, and straight-backed chairs surround a large kitchen table. The adults and children dress in plain colors, and their clothes are often fastened with straight pins. Because buttons are on military uniforms, the Amish will not use them. The Amish have managed to separate themselves from modern values and material things. When visitors see the Amish communities for the first time, they sometimes think they have gone back in time a hundred years.

Other Swiss religious groups have flourished in America as well. Michael Schlatter (1716-1790) organized the German Reform Church of North America, which became one of the largest church groups in America. It eventually joined with the Congregational Church to form the United Church of Christ.

New Glarus

Many other Swiss came to America in the nineteenth century, when major crop failures in Europe drove them to leave their country in search of a better life. Still others left because the new machines of the industrial age replaced their jobs in the textile industry. For many, going to America seemed to offer the hope of a better life.

To Begin Again

On April 15, 1845, 196 citizens from the Swiss canton of Glarus set out on the 7,000-mile (11,200-kilometer) journey to America. Taking only a few clothes and tools, they traveled by foot, wagon, and lakeboat to Basel. Everywhere they went, they were overcharged for food and sleeping quarters.

In Niewaediep, Holland, the Swiss boarded a three-masted sailing ship for America. The ocean voyage was so miserable that a man and three children died. Several storms, rotten potatoes, and very salty food made everybody sick. The small amount of bad water the Swiss had to drink wasn't enough to cleanse the salt out of their bodies.

When they finally docked six weeks later in Baltimore, Maryland, there was little time to celebrate. The men had to unload all the baggage immediately because the captain said he would throw it into the sea if they didn't. The immigrants left Maryland in horse-drawn wagons, heading west. During the journey across America, some people left the group, preferring to settle in other parts of the country and end their travels. By the time the sick and exhausted group reached what is now New Glarus, Wisconsin, only 109 emigrants were left.

Everyone worked hard to develop the colony. Within four years, New Glarus had grown into a thriving, independent community. In 1860, a cheesemaker named Nicklaus Gerber came to New Glarus to make

A log cabin built by an original New Glarus settler.

cheese. Years later, sixty cheese factories were producing huge amounts of American cheese. Although there are no cheese factories in New Glarus anymore, much of today's American cheese is made in Wisconsin, the Dairy State.

Today, the 1,700 people who live in New Glarus have kept much of their Swiss culture. Many can still speak the Glarner dialect that the original settlers spoke. They have also preserved their past in the Swiss Historical Village, which features cheesemaking, print shops with original equipment, and a log cabin. The Hall of History in the village, jointly planned by the people of New Glarus and the Swiss canton of Glarus, opened in 1967. Its first exhibit showed the history of the textile industry in Switzerland. Today, New Glarus has a lace factory that produces embroidery and lace textiles.

Every year, actors and actresses in New Glarus perform the Heidi and William Tell dramas. Since thousands of people go to see those plays, all the hotels in the area have their rooms reserved for more than a year in advance. The stores in New Glarus stock almost as many Swiss souvenirs as Swiss stores do!

Early Swiss Leaders in America

Many Swiss immigrants have made outstanding contributions to the United States. Two of the early ones were Colonel Henry L. Bouquet (1714-1765), who was an officer and an instructor in George Washington's army, and Albert Gallatin (1761-1849). Gallatin was elected to the Pennsylvania legislature, to the United States Senate, and to the House of Representatives. He served as the Secretary of the Treasury in the early 1800s, and later became the United States ambassador to France. He was also a writer, an educator, and a co-founder of New York University.

John Sutter

John Sutter (1803-1880) was very different from many Swiss leaders who came to the United States. He left his wife and child after going bankrupt in Switzerland, and immigrated to the United States in 1834. Sutter settled in Missouri, where he became an unsuccessful trader. Just one step ahead of his creditors, he went to Oregon, and sailed to Hawaii and then on to Alaska. Sutter arrived in California in July 1839. There he received a land grant from the Mexican government of California. It was just farmland then, but today it is Sacramento, the capital of California.

Sutter employed American Indians from a nearby mission to clear the land and dig irrigation ditches for growing wheat. It wasn't long before he had a successful milling, mining, fur trading, and salmon fishing business. In 1841, after seven years of being separated from his wife and son, he brought his family to the United States.

Sutter built a fort that was the western ending point for pioneer wagon trains. When gold was discovered near Sutter's sawmill in 1848, thousands of gold seekers flocked to the area. Soon after the discovery of gold, California became part of the United States, and the next year Sutter was a delegate to the Constitutional Convention of 1849. He was also a candidate in the race

John Sutter played an important role in the early history of California.

to elect the first governor of California. Today the restored Sutter's Fort in Sacramento attracts more than 250,000 visitors every year.

Wittnauer and Ammann

Another important Swiss, Albert Charles Wittnauer (1856-1908), owned a large watch and clock manufacturing company in New York City. His specialty was making high-quality watch cases. Many large companies used Wittnauer clocks for their official timepieces.

A famous Swiss-born man from New York was Othmar Herman Ammann (1879-1965). When he was chief engineer of the Port Authority of New York, he designed the George Washington Bridge, the largest bridge to cross the Hudson River, and the third-longest suspension bridge in the United States.

Louis Chevrolet

A name that many people know is Chevrolet. Louis Chevrolet (1879-1941) was a Swiss race-car driver who came to the United States in 1900. As a member of the Buick racing team, he became associated with William C. Durant, who owned General Motors. Durant gave Chevrolet money to design a good lightweight car to compete with the cars made by Henry Ford. In 1911, Chevrolet produced his first car. He had his own company, but in two years, he sold it to Durant and returned to his greatest love—car racing.

While Durant produced road cars, Chevrolet developed the Frontenas and Monroe racing cars. Seven of his cars were built for the 1920 Indianapolis 500. That year Chevrolet's brother won the race—the first time an American car had won since 1912.

More than a hundred other Swiss have made important contributions to the United States. Though Swiss Americans take the responsibility of their American

A Swiss-American boy and girl dress in folk costumes for a Swiss National Day festival on the first Sunday of August.

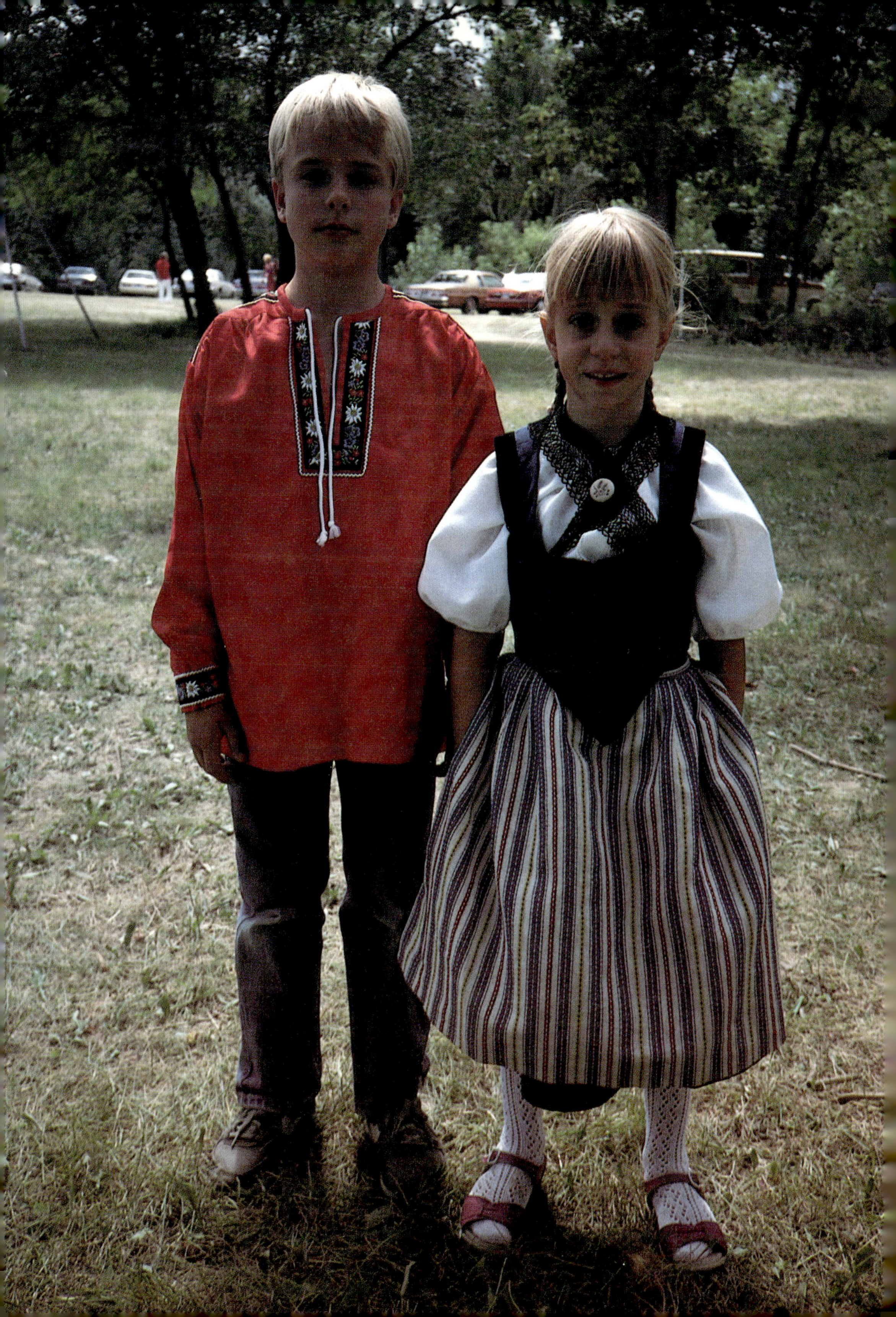

citizenship seriously, the first-generation Swiss continue to have close ties with their native land. Because of an earlier agreement with the United States government, Switzerland is one of the few countries where an immigrant can retain an original citizenship after becoming an American citizen.

Nearly every state has at least one Swiss Club. The clubs were first organized to help other Swiss who were getting started in America. Now they promote their Swiss heritage by taking part in international parades and other celebrations. Most of them hold their Swiss independence day celebration on the first Sunday of August. Folk singing or dancing groups from Switzerland often join in the colorful celebrations.

Even though Swiss Americans are very loyal to their adopted country, they are proud of their heritage. Their rich and varied culture has contributed much to the United States and to American ways of life.

Appendix A
Swiss Cantons

Cantons with Abbreviations:
 Aargau/Argovie (AG)
 Appenzell-Ausserrhoden (AR)
 Appenzell-Innerrhoden (AI)
*Basel-Land (BL)
*Basel-Stadt (BS)
 Bern/Berne (BE)
 Fribourg/Freiburg (FR)
 Genève/Genf/Geneva (GE)
 Glarus/Glaris (GL)
 Graubünden/Grisons (GR)
 Jura (JU)
 Luzern/Lucerne (LU)
 Neuchâtel/Neuenburg (NE)
*Nidwalden (NW)
*Obwalden (OW)
 St. Gallen/St. Gall (SG)
 Schaffhausen/Schaffhouse (SH)
 Schwyz (SZ)
 Solothurn/Soleure (SO)
 Thurgau/Thurgovie (TG)
 Ticino/Tessin (TI)
 Uri (UR)
 Valais/Wallis (VS)
 Vaud/Waadt (VD)
 Zug/Zoug (ZG)
 Zürich/Zurich (ZH)

*half-cantons

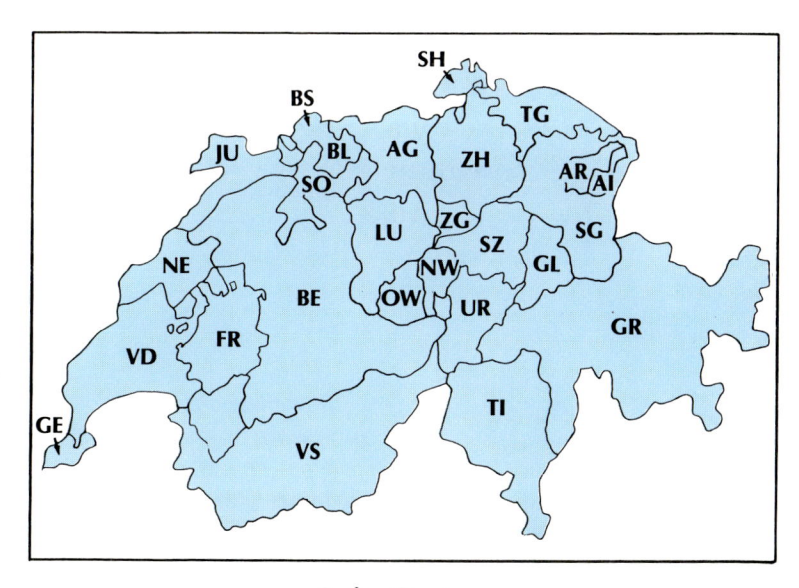

Swiss Cantons

Appendix B

The Official Languages of Switzerland

Switzerland has three official languages: German, French, and Italian. The national newspapers, magazines, and official government papers are printed in these languages. They are not printed in Romansh, another Swiss national language, because only 1 percent of the people speak it. Here are a few phrases and words from Switzerland's official languages.

German

English	German	Pronunciation
Good morning	Guten Morgen	GOOT·en MORG·en
Good evening	Guten Abend	GOOT·en AAB·ent
Good-bye	Auf Wiedersehen	owf VEED·uh·zayen
How are you?	Wie geht es Ihnen?	vee gayt ehs EEN·en
please	bitte	BIT·eh
thank you	danke	DAHNK·eh

French

English	French	Pronunciation
Good morning	Bonjour	bohn·zhoor
Good evening	Bonsoir	bohn·swahr
Good-bye	Au revoir	oh vwahr
How are you?	Comment allez-vous?	koh·mahn tah·lay·voo
please	S'il vous plaît	seel voo pleh
thank you	merci	mehr·see

Italian

English	Italian	Pronunciation
Good morning	Buon giorno	boo·OHN jee·OHR·noh
Good evening	Buona sera	boo·OH·nah SAY·rah
Good-bye	Arrivederci	ahr·ree·veh·DAYR·chee
How are you?	Come sta?	KOH·meh STAH
please	per piacere	PEHR pee·ah·CHAY·reh
thank you	grazie	GRAH·tsee·eh

Appendix C

Swiss Consulates in the United States and Canada

The Swiss embassies and consulates are government offices that want to help the citizens of the United States and Canada understand Swiss ways. They also work with Swiss companies abroad, and they help with any special problems a Swiss might have with citizenship.

United States Consulates and Embassy

Atlanta
Consulate General of Switzerland
1275 Peachtree Street N.E., Suite 425
Atlanta, GA 30309-2176
Phone (404) 872-7874

Chicago
Consulate General of Switzerland
737 N. Michigan Avenue, Suite 2301
Chicago, IL 60611
Phone (312) 915-0061

Houston
Consulate General of Switzerland
Allied Bank Plaza, Suite 5670
1000 Louisiana
Houston, TX 77002
Phone (713) 650-0000

Los Angeles
Consulate General of Switzerland
3440 Wilshire Blvd., Suite 817
Los Angeles, CA 90010
Phone (213) 388-4127

New York
Consulate General of Switzerland
665 Fifth Avenue, Eighth Floor
New York, NY 10022
Phone (212) 758-2560

San Francisco
Consulate General of Switzerland
456 Montgomery Street, Suite 1500
San Francisco, California 94104
Phone (415) 788-2272

Washington, D.C.
Embassy of Switzerland
2900 Cathedral Avenue, N.W.
Washington, D.C. 20008
Phone (202) 745-7900

Canadian Consulates and Embassy

Montreal
  Consulate General of Switzerland
  1572 Dr. Penfield Ave.
  Montreal, Quebec H3G1C4
  Phone (514) 932-7181

Ottawa
  Embassy of Switzerland
  5 Marlborough Avenue
  Ottawa, Ontario K1N8E6
  Phone (613) 235-1837

Toronto
  Consulate General of Switzerland
  1000-100 University Avenue
  Toronto, Ontario M5J1V6
  Phone (416) 593-5371

Vancouver
  Consulate General of Switzerland
  World Trade Center
  790-999 Canada Place
  Vancouver, British Columbia
    V6C3E1
  Phone (604) 684-2231

Glossary

Alps—a mountain range in south central Europe; the largest region of Switzerland
Bahnhofstrasse (BAHN·hohf·strah·seh)—the main street in Zurich
Bärengraben (bayr·ehn·GRAH·behn)—the bear pit in Bern
Basler Leckerli (BAHZ·lur lehk·EHR·lee)—a honey biscuit filled with candied fruit and nuts
Birchermüsli (byr·KAIR·myoos·lee)—a healthy breakfast food containing fruit and nuts developed by Dr. Bircher-Brenner
Bol d' Or (bohl dohr)—"Gold Cup" yacht race held annually on Lake Geneva
Böög (bohg)—"bogeyman"
Bundeshaus (BUHNT·ehs·hows)—the capitol building in Bern
Bürgerbrief (BYOOR·gair·breef)—a miniature citizenship to the Pestalozzi Children's Village
Christkindli (krihs·KIHND·lee)—the Christ Child who comes bearing gifts on Christmas Eve
confiserie (cohn·FEEZ·air·ee)—the French word for dessert shop

Corpus Christi (KOHR·puhs KRIHS·tee)—religious festival in honor of the Eucharist

crèche (krehsh)—the French word for cradle, used to describe a Christmas nativity scene

Diet (DY·eht)—an assembly of princes or estates called together to judge or make decisions

Eierzopf (EYE·air·zahpf)—a large, braided egg bread

Emmentaler (EHM·ehn·tawl·ur)—a kind of Swiss cheese

Fastnacht (FAHS·nahkt)—a carnival in honor of the beginning of Lent

Föhn (furn)—the weather front that brings warm winds and rains to mountain areas

fondue (fahn·DOO)—a popular Swiss cheese dish

Fussball (FOOS·bawl)—the German word for soccer

Gruyère (groo·YAIR)—a kind of Swiss cheese

Gümeli (GYOOM·eh·lee)—potato, in the Swiss German dialect of the canton of Thurgau

Gymnasium (jihm·NAH·zee·uhm)—the academic secondary school that prepares students for a university

Helvetia (hehl·VAYT·see·ah)—the Latin name for Switzerland

Herdöpfel (hair·DURP·fehl)—potato, in another Swiss German dialect

Hochdeutsch (HOHK doych)—high German, or formal German

Hornussen (hohr·NOOS·ehn)—a Swiss sport, often called "farmer's tennis," which is similar to American baseball

Jass (yahs)—a popular Swiss card game

Jura (YOOR·ah)—Switzerland's newest canton (as of 1979); the smallest geographical region of Switzerland

Kinderdorf Pestalozzi (KIHN·dur·dohrf pehs·tah·LOHT·see)—a village for homeless and needy children in the canton of Appenzell

Konditorei (kohn·dee·tohr·EYE)—the German word for dessert shop

Kräbeli (krah·BEH·lee)—aniseed cookies

Landsgemeinde (LAHNTS·gay·myn·day)—an outdoor assembly of people gathered for the purpose of conducting government business

Lehre (LAY·reh)—an apprenticeship to learn a craft or trade

Mardi Gras (MAHR·dee grah)—the French term (meaning "Fat Tuesday") for a festival held on Shrove Tuesday, which is the day before Lent begins

Mehlsuppe (mehl·soo·PEH)—a brown flour soup

Mittelland (MIH·tehl·lahnt)—a region in Switzerland between the Jura Mountains and the Alps; the breadbasket of Switzerland
Nadel (NAH·dehl)—the Romansh word for Christmas
Natale (nah·TAH·lay)—the Italian word for Christmas
Noël (noh·EHL)—the French word for Christmas
Omeletten (ohm·LEHT·tehn)—an egg pancake
Pfingsten (PFIHNG·stehn)—a religious holiday held on the seventh Sunday after Easter; Feast of the Pentecost
polenta (poh·LEHN·tah)—corn meal
Raclette (rah·KLEHT)—a popular cheese dish
Ringli (RIHNG·lee)—doughnutlike cakes
Romansh (roh·MANCH)—an ancient Latin language, spoken by one percent of the Swiss population
Rösti (ROHRS·tee)—fried potatoes
Samiklaus (SAHM·ee·klaws)—Santa Claus
Samiklaus Abend (SAHM·ee·klaws AH·behnd)—Santa Claus Night, celebrated on December 6
Schali (shah·LEE)—Swiss chalet
Schlagball (SHLAG·bawl)—a Swiss game similar to American baseball

Schrebergarten (SHREH·bur·gahr·tehn)—small garden plots in cities that are rented by urban Swiss for family gardens

Schwingen (SHVING·ehn)—Swiss wrestling

Schwyzerdütsch (SHVEET·zur·dootch)—a term given to Swiss German dialect languages

Sechseläuten (sehk·say·LOY·tehn)—an April festival held in honor of the Swiss tradition of guilds; "six o'clock ringing"

Sonderbund (sohn·DUR·buhnd)—a Swiss Catholic government formed in 1845, and dissolved by the Confederation in 1847

Tirggel (TEERG·gehl)—a thin, hard cookie

Unspunnen Stein (oon·SPOON·ehn styn)—a Swiss stone putting or stone-throwing game dating back to 1805

Völkerball (FURL·kur·bawl)—a Swiss game similar to dodge ball

Wanderwege (VAN·dur·vehg·eh)—hiking paths in the mountains

Weihnachten (VY·nahk·tehn)—the German word for Christmas

Znüni (ZSTOO·nee)—a midmorning snack

Selected Bibliography

The Alps. Washington, D.C.: National Geographic Society, Special Publications Division, 1973.

Anderson, Phyl. *Swiss Historical Village, New Glarus, Wisconsin.* New Glarus, WI: New Glarus Historical Society, 1976.

Baedeker's Switzerland. Englewood Cliffs: Prentice-Hall, Inc., 1981.

Hazelton, Nika Standen. *The Swiss Cookbook.* New York: Atheneum, 1973.

Hintz, Martin. *Switzerland: Enchantment of the World.* Chicago: Children's Press, 1986.

Kubly, Herbert. *Native's Return.* New York: Stein and Day Publishers, 1981.

Luck, James Murry. *A History of Switzerland.* Palo Alto, CA; The Society For The Promotion of Science and Scholarship, 1985.

Putman, John J. "The Clockwork Country." *National Geographic.* (January, 1986): 97-126.

Index

acid rain, 57-58
Alemanni, 39
Allies, 52
Alps, 11, 12, 14, 15
Amish, 118, 119, 120
Ammann, Othmar Herman, 126
Anker, Albert, 34
athletic associations: Federal Society of Gymnastics, 108-109; Swiss Rifle Association, 108; Swiss Soccer Association, 108; Youth and Sports, 108
athletic competitions: Bol d'Or (Gold Cup), 115; European World Surfing Championship, 115; Tour de Suisse, 114

Bahnhofstrasse, 18-19
Bärengraben, 18
Basel, 7, 21, 77
Bern, 16, 18, 85
Bernard of Menthon, 12
Bernese Oberland, 68, 88
Biellman, Denise, 117
Biellman spin, 117
Bircher-Brenner (Dr.), 92
Bloch, Ernest, 34
Blümlis Alp, 66, 68
Bouquet, Henry L., 123
Bundeshaus, 16
Bürgerbrief, 107
Burgundians, 39

Caesar, Julius, 38
Calvin, John, 46, 47

cantons: Appenzell, 106; definition of, 18; Fribourg, 44; Nidwalden, 40; Obwalden, 40; Saint Gallen, 112; Schwyz, 40, 42; Solothurn, 44; Thurgau, 112; Ticino, 89; Unterwalden, 40, 43; Uri, 40; Valais, 88, 100
Catholics, 47, 48, 74, 81
Central Powers, 52
Charlemagne, 40, 64-65
Charles the Bold, 44
cheese: cheesemaking, 95-96; Emmentaler, 97; *fondue*, 97-98; Gruyère, 97; *Raclette*, 98
Chernobyl, 58-59
Chevrolet, Louis, 126
Ciba-Geigy, 21
Congress of Vienna, 48
Council of Europe, 54

Devil's Bridge, 68-69
Diet, 44
Dunant, Jean-Henri, 50

eternal pact, 40, 42
European Trade Association, 54

Federal Assembly, 16, 18
Federal Council, 18
Ferdinand, Archduke Francis, 51-52
Föhn, 12-13
food: *Basler Leckerli*, 100; beverages, 95; *Birchermüsli*, 92; for breakfast, 91; chocolate, 20, 79, 98; coffee, 91-92; *confiserie*, 99; desserts, 99; *Eierzopf*, 92-93; *Kartoffelrösti* recipe, 94-95; *Konditorei*, 99; *Krabeli*, 100;

Mehlsuppe, 79; for noon meal, 93, 94; *Omeletten*, 95; *Ringli*, 100; *Rösti*, 94; soup, 94-95; for supper, 95; *Tirggel*, 100; *Znüni*, 98

Gallatin, Albert, 123
Geneva, 7, 20, 38, 46
Geneva, Lake, 20, 38, 102, 115
Gerber, Nicklaus, 121-122
German Reform Church, 120
Gessler, 60-64
Gorbachev-Reagan summit, 55
Graubünden, 27
Great Saint Bernard Pass, 12, 38

Habsburgs, 40, 42, 60
Heidi, 36, 123
Heidi Alp, 36
Heimatwerk, 30
Helvetian Republic, 48
Helvetians, 38
Hess, Erika, 115-116
Hitler, Adolf, 53
Hodler, Ferdinand, 34
holidays: Advent, 74; Ash Wednesday, 77; *Böögg*, burning of the, 83; *Christkindli*, 76; Christmas, 76, 100; Corpus Christi, 81; *crèche*, 74; Easter, 79; *Fastnacht* Carnival, 77; Lent, 77, 79; onion festival, 85; *Pfingsten* (Pentecost), 79; *Samiklaus*, 74-76; *Samiklaus Abend*, 74; *Sechseläuten*, 81; William Tell Festival, 84
Holy Roman Empire, 40, 45

Honegger, Arthur, 34
Huns, 39

Inn (river), 14
International Labor Organization, 54
International Red Cross, 50, 51

Jass, 31, 88
Jews, 49
Jung, Carl, 31-33
Jura, 11, 12, 21
Jura Mountains, 11, 21

Kinderdorf Pestalozzi, 106
Klee, Paul, 34

Landsgemeinde, 29
League of Nations, 53
League of Red Cross Societies, 50
Lehmann, Peter, 118
Leopold III, Duke, 42, 43
Locarno, 14
Lucerne, Lake, 40, 60
Lugano, 14
Luther, Martin, 46

Mennonites, 118-119
Mittelland, 11, 15, 16
Morgarten, 42, 43, 84
Müller, Peter, 116

Nadel, 74
Napoleon Bonaparte, 48

Natale, 74
Neanderthals, 37
Neuchâtel, 22
neutrality: adoption of, 48; current policy of, 8; defense and, 55; United Nations and, 54; von Flüe and, 45; World War I and, 51; World War II and, 53
New Glarus, Wisconsin: cheesemaking in, 121-122; contemporary life in, 122; emigrants to, 120-121; Swiss Historical Village in, 122
Noel, 74

Olympic Games, winter, 115-116

Palace of Nations, 20, 53
Penn, William, 118
Pestalozzi, Johann Heinrich, 104-106
Pestalozzidorf, 106-107
Piaget, Jean, 31, 33
polenta, 91
Protestantism, 46
Protestants, 47, 48, 74

Reformation, 46
Rhaeti, 38
Rhine (river), 14, 21, 59
Rhône (river), 14, 20
Romans, 38, 39
Romansh, 10, 27, 39
Rossini, Gioacchino, 64
Rousseau, Jean-Jacques, 33
Rütli, 40, 42

Saint Gotthard Pass, 12
Sandoz warehouse, 59
Schali (chalet), 88
Schantz, Joseph, 118
Schlatter, Michael, 120
Schneider, Vreni, 117
schools: field trips and, 102; grading in, 101-102; *Gymnasium*, 103; hours of, 101; learning languages in, 102; *Lehre*, 103-104; primary level of, 101; public systems of, 104; secondary level of, 101; studying and, 101; Swiss Institute of Technology, 20; University of Zurich, 20
Schreber, Daniel, 87
Schrebergarten, 87-88
Segantini, Giovanni, 34
Simmons, Menno, 118
Sonderbund War, 49, 50
sports: bicycling, 114; boating, 114-115; *Fussball* (soccer), 108; gymnastics, 109; hiking, 31, 114; *Hornussen*, 110; horseback riding, 112; *Schlagball*, 111-112; *Schwingen*, 110; skiing, 13, 115; *Unspunnen Stein*, 110; *Völkerball*, 112
Spyri, Johanna, 36
Stone Age, 37
Strategic Arms Limitations talks (SALT I and II), 55
stucco, 89
Stückelberger, Christine, 112-113
Sutter, John, 124-125
Swiss clubs, 128
Swiss Confederation, 42, 44, 48, 49

Swiss Family Robinson, 36
Swiss French, 36, 71, 102
Swiss Germans, 27, 70, 86, 102
Swiss Italians, 26, 71, 102
Swiss National Day, 42, 128
Switzerland: banks in, 19; boys' roles in, 86, 87; business in, 21; citizenship in, 24-25, 128; crafts in, 30; farming in, 38; farmland of, 15; girls' roles in, 86; government of, 16, 18; homemaking in, 27; homeowners in, 88; houses in, 88-91; hydroelectric power in, 14; industry in, 20, 21; as international meeting ground, 24; kitchens in, 91; languages spoken in, 10, 26; men's roles in, 29; military in, 56; military fortification of, 56; music in, 34, 84; nuclear power in, 14, 58; pollution in, 56-57; president of, 18; tourists in, 20, 58; trade in, 21; traditional costumes of, 81; urbanization in, 88; visual art in, 33, 34; watchmaking in, 22; women's rights in, 28; women's roles in, 27-28

Tell, William, 7, 60-64, 123

Third Reich, 53
Ticino (river), 14
Treaty of Versailles, 52

United Nations, 20, 54
UNESCO (United Nations Educational, Scientific, and Cultural Organization), 54

von Flüe, Niklaus, 44, 45
Von Schiller, Friedrich, 64, 84
von Winkelreid, Arnold, 43

Wanderwege, 31
Weinachten, 74
Witz, Konratt, 34
Wittnauer, Albert Charles, 125
World War I, 50, 52
World War II, 53-54, 106
Wyss, Johann David, 34-36

Zurbriggen, Pirmin, 116
Zurich, 7, 18-19, 20, 81
Zwingli, Huldreich, 46

About the Author

Margaret Schrepfer, who is married to a Swiss, has traveled extensively throughout Switzerland. She has written several articles for publications such as the *Swiss American Review*. In addition to her writing, she has worked in Michigan as an elementary school teacher and a private tutor. The author currently resides in Haslett, Michigan.

J 949.4 S   C.1
Schrepfer, Margaret.
   Switzerland, the summit of
Europe
                         12.95

DATE DUE

JAMES PRENDERGAST LIBRARY ASSOCIATION

JAMESTOWN, NEW YORK

Member Of

Chautauqua-Cattaraugus Library System